Adventures in Shroomville

The Mystery of Hedgehog Hill

*For Mason : I hope you
enjoy my book...*

Ron Dennis

Ron Dennis

Manor House

Library and Archives Canada
Cataloguing in Publication

Dennis, Ron, 1945-
The mystery of Hedgehog Hill : adventures in Shroomville / Ron
Dennis.

ISBN 978-1-897453-32-2

I. Title.

PS8607.E672M97 2010   jC813'.6   C2010-907093-3

Printed and bound in Canada
First Edition.
144 pages.

Cover design: Michael B. Davie and Donovan Davie
We gratefully acknowledge use of cover illustration: courtesy of
artist Stephen M. Dennis

Published October 30, 2010
Manor House Publishing Inc.

We gratefully acknowledge the financial support of the
Government of Canada through Book Fund Canada, Dept. of
Canadian Heritage.

Manor House Publishing Inc.
www.manor-house.biz
905-648-2193

For my brother Steve, whose 1970s drawings of mushroom villages, sparked this book. For sons Geoff and Kevin, who continue to inspire.

Prologue

For as long as memory – until recently, that is – Shroomville had been a happy little village, tucked away deep in a vast boreal forest whose bristling green canopy stretched beyond forever.

Villagers went about their daily business, growing food, (their main crops were oats, barley, rice and several varieties of berries) or tending flocks of sheep and goats. They also kept busy repairing wagons and tools, weaving cloth, sewing clothing, fashioning all manner of household articles, building sheds – even writing books and educating the young ones.

Oh, one little detail makes this village stand out. You see, these villagers are tiny... about as tall as a typical adult's size-nine shoe. And they live peacefully and happily in mushroom houses. Large, living mushroom houses.

Twisting lazily through the village, its streets are lined with all manner of cozy mushroom homes – each with its own mossy quilt of lawn front and back. Huge trees tower so high, their tops can barely be glimpsed. And for a few of the older villagers, it was a good walk to circle some of the trees' massive trunks.

At the centre of town stands a wooden gazebo, its eight-sided shape surrounded by a stout picket railing over which stood a sheltering, conical, mushroom roof.

Encircling this structure were steps, then a broad expanse of lawn and then Shroom Avenue with its shops.

On the lawn stood swings and jungle-gyms alongside sandboxes where generations of Shroomville children have played under the watchful eyes of their parents.

Tiny though it was, Shroomville seemed to exist under an invisible dome that hid and protected it from the wild denizens of the forest, not to mention the big people who occasionally drew near. So the people of Shroomville and their living, growing, mushroom dwellings thrived for generation after generation – happy with their families... content with their lives.

Recently, however, the village's consistently fine weather seemed to be getting quirky; too often, it seemed, blue skies turned black with great swaths of jagged lightening and sheets of pelting rain. Worse yet, Shroomvillagers had begun to feel the occasional tremor shake their dwellings and shops, rattling dishes and upsetting their calm existence.

Along with the odd tremors and more-than-usual bad weather, some in the village began to sense a kind of foreboding – a nameless fear of something they knew not.

It all started two months earlier, when Shroomville's Town Constable disappeared while searching for a young girl who had become lost. The two had never returned and time – eight long weeks – led a few to link their vanishing with the ominous changes in nature's cycles.

Most, however, shrugged off the tremors and strange weather as the natural order of things. "After all," village barber 'Clip' Tonsorial ventured to anyone who would listen – and most in his captive, one-chair audience, did – "this little patch of weird weather could be just a hiccup in history."

So life continued mostly as always along Shroomville's tidy streets lined with well-kept homes and shops, surrounded by neatly trimmed gardens and lush, mossy lawns.

Mostly as always...

For the few, the mystery never died. For instance, the daily cycle of sun and darkness never passed without the Constable's wife and son wondering what had happened to their husband and father... and the lad's best friend, Portia Bella, who lived down the street.

The village teacher and lore-keeper also continued to wonder. More than that, his sense of dread continued to grow.

"Somehow, sometime," Phinneus T. Phungi thought, stroking a grey hedge of ragged whiskers "we'll all find out what happened... and the events surrounding that eye-opener won't be pleasant!"

1

The strange dream

For the umpteen generations since Shroomville was settled by Marshall Shroom's Great-Many Grandfather, few had ever explored the twisting, root-gnarled path as it meandered its way up Hedgehog Hill.

That was about to change, Marshall murmured – all first-born boys in his family were named Marshall, or Mars, to family and friends – as he crept quietly through an old shantytown at the base of Hedgehog Hill. Once a kind of countrified, offshoot village of Shroomville, the shantytown was more spread out... more old fashioned.

Now, however, the town looked more like a messy bedroom, houses and shops strewn everywhere. There was also a smell of decay and a look of total neglect. Its houses and shops, like those in Shroomville, were living things.

Except with its mostly orange-capped roofs and ramshackle living quarters, the shantytown was mysteriously deserted. No one knew why and no one rushed to set up house there – so powerful was the feeling of... of... Well Mars didn't know what the feeling was but he knew he didn't like it.

Now, there were no sounds of children playing… no busy shops… no villagers scuttling to and fro doing their daily business.

"Been that way for longer than most anyone remembers," Mars shivered involuntarily, running his fingers through a thatch of carrot-red hair. "One day I'll find out why."

For most of his nearly 13 years, Mars had given free rein to a natural – some would say, intense – curiosity. Like all youngsters, he first pulled himself to his feet, exulting in the new vistas that opened up. Learning to walk consisted of leaning in the direction he wanted to go and then letting little rubbery legs try to catch up.

At first, it was more tumble than toddle. But soon, balance arrived and stout legs obeyed their owner… at least to some degree.

Soon too, he began to explore his own bright and cheery home. He discovered first the pure joy of seeing and discovering a new room… then a new view out one of its windows. He also discovered how painful it could be when a trip at the top of the stairs led to what seemed like unending bouncing bumps and scrapes to the bottom.

As he grew older, Mars noticed some other oddities about himself.

Like when he was reading in bed and heavy lidded, pale-blue eyes were about to slam shut, he'd carefully mark his page, place the book on his bedside table and with a "f-f-wit," the candle would sputter out.

All by itself!

Other times, just when he seemed to think about a fire in the hearth, it would blaze into flame… or lamps would flare into life when he strode into a darkened room.

"Curious," admitted his father – scratching his own thatch of slightly greying red hair – when Mars pressed for answers. "But I'd say they were curious coincidences."

Then he'd quickly change the subject.

That didn't stop Mars. Of all Shroomville children, Mars was, by far, the most inquisitive. He needed to know.

Know what was under the bed in his parents' room…
Know what was in that kitchen cupboard high above the sink…
Know what lurked in the basement behind that stout, usually locked door…

And in almost fearless fashion, he'd found the answers to most of these questions, one way or another. Now, Mars was about to know something else – know something that no one else in Shroomville seemed to know. He was about to know what was at the top of the Hedgehog Hill trail that snaked up and beyond the deserted shantytown.

He crept carefully through the creepy old town, past its broken-down gazebo and run-down shops and homes, pausing briefly to read the "Apothecary" sign off in the distance, his eye drawn to it by the oddly, bright yellow door leading into the establishment.

He started up the hill past the ancient, dilapidated general store at the edge of the deserted town, every so often looking behind and from side to side… just in case.

The crest of the hill loomed closer and closer and Mars began to tremble, brushing aside curiously curled vines as he climbed.

The twisty trail wound left and right – even doubling back on itself – and the vines seemed to rustle and twist around his ankles as if they wanted to snare him and stop his progress.

That's when he heard the strangely hollow voice. Even stranger because it was, somehow, familiar. He stopped suddenly, cupping hands behind ears to hear more clearly.

"Marshall," the voice called out sweetly, echoing as if it were coming from the bottom of a well.
"Marshall…

"It's time to get up," his mother called, gently rapping on his bedroom door. "You don't want to be late for school on the last day before summer holidays."

Visions of Hedgehog Hill and the decaying shanty town below it vanished like morning mist on the meadow.

But the urge Mars felt to see what lay beyond the crest of Hedgehog Hill, did not. And what better time could there be to satisfy that curiosity than the lazy days of summer?

Somehow, whatever was there, was connected to his father's and Portia Bella's disappearance, he thought, a sudden sadness washing over him.

"And I intend to find out!" he promised himself.

2

The quest begins

Mars wasn't entirely sure why he awoke that last-day-of-school morning, feeling anxious... hands still cupped behind ears, but he wasn't alarmed. Snatches of his dream darted in and out of his head as he jumped from bed into slippers, dashing to wash the sleep from his eyes and brush his teeth.

For some reason – he didn't know exactly why – the dream bits shone a ray of hope into the heavy gloom of sorrow and unhappiness he'd been wearing for two long months... hope that he'd once again see his father and Portia.

Somehow, he knew his father and Portia were still alive. It was a feeling that burned brighter that morning, casting aside the shadows of their disappearance.

Back in his room, he stripped off pyjamas and donned the regular school clothes laid neatly at the foot of his bed. Today, it was a sturdy, pale brown pull-over shirt to accompany the dark green pants he often wore.

"Did it have something to do with the haunting voice from his dream, the one that morphed into his mother's cheery wake-up call?" he asked himself as he shrugged into his wide, white and green-striped suspenders. Still musing over his dream, he ran downstairs and sat at the kitchen table.

From the time he could speak, Mars was known among family, friends – and teachers – for asking a lot of questions. Some thought he was a bit nosy. Others just thought he was, well, a bit strange.

But quite often, to the amazement of older Shroomvillagers and teachers, he found his own answers after thinking it through.

Problem was, when puzzling over a particularly thorny question, Mars looked like he was daydreaming... pale blue eyes barely open and gazing far off.

Just like now.

"Marshall," said his mother, "you haven't touched your breakfast. Better get moving or you'll be late for school."

With that, Mars carefully tucked thoughts away, knowing he'd revisit them later, and tucked into the hearty bowl of oatmeal, topped with blueberries, brown sugar and cream that lay before him. It was his favourite breakfast.

With the last mouthful, he noticed the small, bright yellow, carefully wrapped packet under the overhang of his bowl. He snatched it up and turned excitedly to his mother.

"I thought you had forgotten," he said, grinning broadly, blue eyes now open wide... silently entreating permission to open the packet.

"How could I forget your thirteenth birthday," his mother smiled. "It's the most important one of all... But you know how we do this every year. You don't open your present until you're home from school. So off you go."

Then it was another quick wash-up and teeth-brushing, before grabbing his backpack – jammed with the hearty lunch his mother had packed and all the reading material he would shortly return to the library on that last day of school.

Though her own sorrow at the mysterious disappearance of her husband was almost too much to bear, Marshall's mother tried mightily to maintain at least the appearance of a normal life for her only son. So as always, she stood patiently at the open door.

Smiling and smoothing her crisply starched apron, she opened her arms for the daily hug-'n-run they shared. Taller than his mother now, Mars was too big to scoop up and cuddle, so she braced to receive the quick squeeze as her son ran out the door.

Today's embrace was just a bit heartier than normal, she thought, straightening her apron-covered red gingham dress and smoothing the dark brown hair that was drawn up neatly behind and tied with a matching gingham ribbon.

If only Marshall Senior were here, she thought, tears welling as Mars ran down the street. He'd be so proud...

But Marshall Senior hadn't been seen in Shroomville for two long months. He'd vanished one morning when his duties as Town Constable had taken him to Hedgehog Hill, she recalled, pale hazel eyes misting. She missed him so...

The events of that day washed over her once again. The Constable had gone out in search of young Portia, the pretty, precocious daughter of Peter and Pamela Bella. Always known as adventurous, Portia had headed out on her own exploration mission and strangely, didn't return.

Both fiercely independent, smart as a whips and quick to laugh, Portia and Mars had been nearly inseparable since they were toddlers. Energetic and strong, Portia easily outran, out-climbed and outsmarted all of the village girls... and many village boys. She was even close to a match for Mars...

Close, but not quite...

The pair did almost everything together. They explored the paths that criss-crossed Shroomville and climbed trees to see as far as they could see. They whittled sticks and sometimes, just sat on the bridge that arched over Criminy Creek, dangling feet in the burbling waters and talking.

They were, in short, as close as close could be. When villagers saw Mars, nine times out of ten, they also saw Portia… the two of them simply enjoying each other's company.

One day, however, Portia found herself at loose ends and struck out on a hike alone.

No one really knew what it was, but that day, something piqued her curiosity and lured her to Hedgehog Hill.

Something compelling…
Something irresistible…

Marshall Senior painstakingly searched the village; he soon found traces of the girl's trail, pointing toward the shantytown and Hedgehog Hill. He followed the trail and like Portia, he too vanished later that day.

Strangely, right about when villagers felt the Constable likely disappeared, the sky over Shroomville darkened and filled with jagged bolts of lightening – red lightening – accompanied by ear-shattering claps of thunder.

With two mysterious disappearances and the eerie storm, the rest of the villagers soon thought it best not to risk any further vanishings and the search was abandoned. Such was the sense of danger and foreboding that clung like cobwebs to Hedgehog Hill.

But young Mars never stopped wondering what happened to his father and Portia, his closest friend. And though their disappearance weighed heavily, he never stopped believing that one day, he'd find them.

It was in Mars' nature to be positive. Though he missed Portia and was quieter without her, his nimble mind worked without rest trying to figure out how and why she disappeared... and how and why his father too, disappeared.

Well, his mother thought, dabbing at her eyes with an apron corner, that's all burbles beneath the bridge. Time to clean up the kitchen and make the beds...

Right at that exact same moment, young Mars had his first serious – really serious – daydream. Not that all his other mind-drifts, as he liked to call them, were unimportant ... they weren't.

This one was different. It was also pretty creepy and more than a bit chilling.

After all, Mars thought later, how often do images of a missing father and best friend flash across the mind's eye with such clarity it seemed like a message from the great beyond.

Yet there they were, communicating with him as if they were in the same room together. He could see them plainly. While he heard their voices and saw Portia blinking tears from her eyes, strangely, their lips did not move. Mars wasn't sure, but he thought he detected a framework surrounding his father and Portia... criss-crossed bars fashioned from stout wood or metal.

Right then, Mars was walking the five short blocks to Shroomville Academy and trying to cope with a monumental mind-drift – one unlike any he'd ever experienced. Though nothing was said, he knew it had something to do with the shantytown and the mysterious hill that lay beyond it; he knew he had to remember every little detail.

He knew there was a clue about what lay up the tortuous path beyond that abandoned village and that somehow, it had something to do with his best friend, Portia, who he missed almost as much as his father.

The father who taught him so much… the father who patiently showed him how to fish, grilled him about healing herbs in the forest and patiently, wisely, thoroughly answered the boy's seemingly endless questions.

The father he missed so terribly at a time in his life when he had so many more questions.

Mrs. Crimini, the town dressmaker, Mr. White, who ran the Shroomville General Store and even the richest man in town – Artemus Trufflemonger – all saw Mars and his glazed-eye march that last day of school.

They gave it little heed; they'd seen young Mars drift off before. Indeed, Mars' mind-drifts often evoked knowing nods and bemused smiles among Shroomville adults…

Mars' teacher, the bewhiskered, bespectacled Phinneas T. Phungi, was perhaps the one who best knew the boy's flights of fancy. Even he gave that glassy-eyed shamble and lack of response to his own hearty "good morning," little more than a passing thought as he cycled past the lad on his own way to school.

Phinneas T. Phungi – wearing his usual rumpled tweed jacket – was the oldest and most respected man in town. No one knew how old he was. Some joked that he was "older than dirt."

More than the other villagers, the portly old man knew there was something special about young Marshall Shroom. More than even the boy's mother, he knew Mars was gifted and had a destiny to fulfil.

Besides his teaching duties, Phungi was Shroomville's lore collector. He made it his business to gather and teach, the town's history, traditions and the roles some of its forebears played in it. He knew much about Shroomville, in particular why all its Town Constables were named Marshall Shroom. And why the job passed from one to the next first-born male.

But that bit, the craggy old man could share only with first-born Shrooms named Marshall. And only on or after their 13th birthdays. And only, in this case, because Marshall Senior wasn't there to take on this vital task.

"I'd much rather the Constable were here to explain things to his son," Phungi thought to himself as he pedalled past Mars. "But I made a promise…"

Unlike the rest of his students, young Mars not only soaked up this history, he asked questions. Questions that seemed deeper, more mature than the boy's years.

Questions that made old Phungi's already furrowed brow crease in concentration, before he cautiously answered. Responses had to be measured until Mars reached age 13.

Still and all, no one, not even Phungi, noted that Mars' typically open gait was a bit more purposeful than usual as he passed from sight.

And no one saw Mars pause, then swerve to the left onto Bran Street, when the leafy, tree-canopied right fork – Academy Lane – led to the school.

Just 30 minutes later, however, everyone noticed when young Marshall was late on that last day of school before the summer holidays.

Marshall didn't give it a thought. All he knew was this mind-drift was more than a flight of fancy. It was a pointed message and he sat on a rock beside the well-worn path leading over Crimini Creek toward Hedgehog Hill to ponder it.

And commit it to memory!

An hour after the opening bell pealed on that last day of school, everyone in town knew Mars was missing. Strangely, two months to the day after his father and Portia Bella disappeared!

Oddly… on Marshall's 13th birthday!

Two hours later, some villagers found the books from Mars' backpack, neatly stacked and sheltered under a makeshift leaf-tarp beside the rock where he pondered that bizarre vision.

That's when the debate on whether to search beyond Crimini Creek, quickly ended when not a single villager volunteered to join a search party. Such was the malevolent atmosphere that seemed to hover over the abandoned shantytown and Hedgehog Hill.

Three hours later, tears flowed once more in the Shroom household. Tears of anguish for a lost son. Tears of anger against a town that was unable to overcome its collective fear.

Tears of a wife and mother who was now, totally alone.

Yet somehow in her heart, after talking with old Phungi, there sprang a faint ray of hope.

Together, they reasoned that her son was on some kind of vital quest that only he could take on.

A quest that held some hope for the return of all three…

It was all she could cling to…

3

The apothecary

For the past six months, Mars had been noticing little changes about himself. Not the regular changes like growing quickly out of clothing or trying to control a voice that seemed to warble from child's to man's – and back again – of its own accord.

No, these changes were almost imperceptible and unexplainable. In recent months, for instance, what his father had earlier dismissed as "curious coincidence," seemed to become highly predictable.

As he read by candlelight before sleep, he noticed something strange. As eyelids drooped, he'd mark the page and close his book, as usual. Now, however, by focusing even his waning attention on the candle, its flame would quickly flutter out... by itself!

When he approached doors with hands full of wood for the fire, or books from the library, a similar focus of attention would cause them to swing open. All by themselves.

But strangest of all were the dreams he could barely remember the instant he woke up... dreams in which his father and Portia seemed to be trying to reach him. Today, on his 13th birthday, came a waking mind-drift much like his dreams, but much clearer – and far more powerful.

"Marshall," two faintly familiar voices in his head softly murmured. "We need to come home. We can't hold out much longer. You have to help us."

Seconds later, images of the shantytown flooded his mind.

That's when Mars took the left fork – the one leading to Hedgehog Hill – instead of the right one leading to the elegantly named Shroomville Academy. His feet seemed to have a mind of their own as they pulled him toward the old shantytown across the meadow, over Crimini Creek and through Fern Forest from Shroomville.

As he marched across Morel meadow and along the edge of Fern Forest, more images flowed unbidden into his mind. Mars didn't know what they meant or where they came from, but he knew they were somehow important and tried to remember as much detail as he could.

One of them, a dilapidated old shroom-shack with a conical windswept roof, sagging shutters, windows opaque with dust and, curiously, a bright yellow door standing slightly ajar, seemed vital. Somehow, he knew it was a key starting point.

Somehow his feet knew too, because they led him over Crimini Creek, through Fern Forest and into the ramshackle town below Hedgehog Hill.

Those feet kept moving Mars right past rows of deserted homes and shops – shutters askew, porches in ruins, windows nearly grown over – right to the village square with its tumbledown gazebo. The playground that surrounded it was now overgrown with weeds that almost hid the rotting swings and see-saws that once amused the town's children.

What was once a pretty, well-cropped, tidy village heath was now anything but. Weeds bristled and vines crawled everywhere, seeming to choke whatever life there had ever been from the shantytown. Everywhere was the dank odour of desolation and disuse.

How many little kids must have played here, Mars thought. He could visualize parents pushing delighted children higher and higher on swings that now stood idle and rusting, some of their seats broken in half.

Mostly, he wondered, "Why am I here?" as he picked his way through the overgrown playground.

Even though it was almost mid-morning, the sun didn't seem to light up the bedraggled village the way it should. It was there, all right, but somehow fainter – as if reflecting off a poorly silvered mirror or shining through a dirty window. By the time any light made it through the trees, ferns and gnarled old vines that seemed to be everywhere, it was like twilight on a gloomy day.

Mars could barely make it out, but a glimmer of colour caught his eye. A shimmer of yellow, actually. He turned past the old well, skirted the dilapidated gazebo with its crumbling, moss-covered, wooden steps and broken railing and soon stood before an old building with windswept roof, grown-over windows and yellow door.

It was the one from his vision.

Mars' feet moved again… this time they marched him straight toward that yellow door, stopping abruptly about an arm's-length away. Above the rounded portal, Mars squinted up to make out an arc of faded, weather-beaten lettering he could barely see. It read: P - - n - i's Apothecary.

He knew that an apothecary was really an old word for pharmacy. That was where his mother went to get the potions and herbs that helped calm his upset stomach or brought down the swelling from an insect sting or healed a bramble-bush scratch.

But what was that first word? It looked like someone's name. Perhaps the name of the shopkeeper. The mind that some said drifted a bit too much, suddenly spit out the answer and it stopped Mars in his tracks.

"Phungi! It has to be Phungi," Mars blurted out loud, his voice sounding strangely hollow and definitely alone.

It suddenly came back to him… the day he found the old teacher's journal – what Phinneas T. Phungi called his "Lore Log." The day he read about, or was about to read about, the village near Hedgehog Hill. The day he was about to find out what had happened to this little town that no one would speak about.

The bad news was, that's also where curious Mars found the last entry in Phungi's Lore Log. The last entry was exactly two months ago… the day Marshall Senior – the Town Constable – disappeared in his search for his friend Portia Bella.

All of these previously unconnected details came together Eureka-like in the boy's mind. But what did the yellow door have to do with it all? he wondered.

"Something important is behind that door," he muttered to himself. "I need to know what it is."

That's when another strange thing happened. With all that wondering and thinking about this bright, though decaying portal, the yellow door suddenly swung open a few inches – rusted hinges groaning.

Mars jumped back in alarm. And as he stood, still wondering what lay beyond, the yellow door flung itself wide open.

Eyes wider than winter coat-buttons, Mars shuddered as he peered through the door past dust-strings and cobwebs, trying to penetrate the gloom.

He had to go in. There were just too many questions. He had to know the answers.

Squaring his shoulders and straightening his shirt, Mars plunged forward into the gloom.

4

The gift

Brushing aside cobwebs and dust-strings, (Mars shuddered as they dragged across his forehead and cheeks), he stepped past the yellow door and into a room of almost unimaginable murkiness. Good thing for Mars, he always carried a few special items in his backpack. One of those items was what he called his living-light-bottle.

Awhile back, he'd saved a firefly nest, ironically, from a gust of wind that blew tongues of flame toward it from a campfire. And though they didn't speak to him, the glowing little bugs had somehow let him know they'd always be with him if he needed light. Mars never told anyone about the incident because, well, it was just too weird.

Yet when he needed light, they somehow appeared in his light-bottle, collectively casting a yellow-green glow, thrusting a plume of light into the dusty darkness.

He crept past a long, high, glassed-in counter that displayed dozens of oddly shaped bottles and tiny boxes – each with its own label. There were remedies for colds, herbs for poultices and whole cabinets filled with various kinds of incense for everything from inducing relaxation to curing headaches.

He caught names like Bloodroot, Woodwart, Wild Ginger, Pepper Root, Spearmint, Five-Finger Grass and Dandelion.

Atop the high counter, Mars could barely make out what appeared to be a row of once-shiny-now dusty, earthenware bowls ranging from small to quite large, each with its own stout stoneware pestle for crushing, grinding and blending the herbs.

At the end, in a small, doorless office behind the counter, Mars stumbled across a massive oaken roll-top desk.

He stood before it, firefly lantern held high, searching for a keyhole or other means to unlock and open the old roll-top. Somehow he knew that something important lay inside it – another clue, perhaps.

Again, it happened. By merely thinking deeply about the multi-slatted roll-top, it defied gravity and slowly snaked upward along its curved tracks and disappeared into the desk. But if that was a surprise, what lay behind the ingeniously crafted wooden slats was truly astonishing.

As the desk-cover slowly rolled up, a faint light spilled from its interior – the kind of odd luminosity that comes just after a thunder and lightening storm. Try as he might, Mars could spot no source for the sheen. It just seemed to be there.

Well, at least he could give his friendly fireflies a rest, he thought. As he always did, he murmured "Thanks, guys," and returned the living lantern to the dark folds of his backpack.

Pulling an old oak armchair closer, he blew off a cloud of dust, climbed atop its seat and peered down at the expanse of desktop with its vertical bank of almost uncountable drawers, large and small. That's when a verse – or at least all but one line – appeared like a fine contrasting inlay on the desk's surface.

It was a verse his father used to sing to him each night at bedtime, encouraging a then-young Mars to learn it by heart. And though Mars hadn't thought about it for a very long time – he considered it just an amusing nonsense rhyme to lull him to sleep – the words and memories of the warm, comforting arms of his father flooded back.

"Mares eat oats
And does eat oats
And little lambs, eat ivy…" which is where the inlaid verse ended... short of the follow up verse:

Except Mars remembered it this way…
 "Mairzy dotes
And dosey dotes
And little lambzy dyvies…"
Reaching deep into a storehouse of bittersweet memories of his father, Mars quickly recalled the last line: "A kiddley divey too, wouldn't you?"

He never really knew what the words meant but loved singing the rhythmic nonsense with his father as bedtime eyelids grew heavy. Now he could read and understand the words of the first three lines but how did that fourth line really read?

Mars thought some more and soon that nimble mind spat out the answer: "A kid'll eat ivy too, wouldn't you?" he thought. Then, reaching out instinctively, he "wrote" the line on the desk with his forefinger.

The peculiar light seemed to shimmer and a shiny, mirror-like rectangle slowly rose from an unseen slot in the middle of the desk's writing surface. Like a moth drawn to a candle, Mars' hand reached out to touch the surface of the strange metal.

At his touch, even stranger things happened. The metal glowed brightly and changed colour. Instead of reflecting his image, it became a window, through which he could barely make out the shape of another person.

And despite the fact that person's face was turned away, it was oddly familiar shape...

"Who's there," came the gravelly voice of the image, as he turned slowly to face the window. "Who could possibly know the words?"

"That voice," thought Mars. "I know that voice!"

He stared intently at the window as the image sharpened and the shape swivelled into view. There sat a craggy, bearded Phinneas T. Phungi – bushy eyebrows bristling over glinting spectacles – also staring intently at his own "window" to see who had summoned him.

Though only short seconds, it seemed like minutes as incredulity strained at the two who communicated by magic window.

"It's you!" the two said almost in unison. But then old Phungi took it one step further.

"Somehow, I knew I should hurry home," he said, polishing his spectacles and replacing them on his nose. "When I heard they found your books at the path-fork, with your footprints leading to Hedgehog Hill, something made me think I might hear from you.

"And now that you've found the 'talk-window' I know at last that you indeed, are a true elder Shroom," Phungi continued. "Because it's only first-born Shrooms who have the gift. I only have a bit of it because your father felt it might be useful one day."

"But how... why... what gift are you talking about," Mars interrupted. This was all happening too fast for him to grasp.

"The gift is not easy to explain," the old man replied, straightening his familiar navy blue sweater-vest beneath a rumpled grey tweed jacket and removing his spectacles to polish them again.

"As far as I can find out, it started with your Great-Many Grandfather Shroom, who founded our little village.

All I know is he had the gift and all first-born Shrooms have it too.

"It's why you all are destined to be the Shroomville Village Constable. Not because we have a lot of crime here – you know perfectly well we don't – but the Constable does play a vital role in protecting and preserving our way of life.

"It would take too long to explain it all now," Phungi said, a note of urgency creeping into his voice. "If you grab onto both sides of the talk-window, its powers will help fill in at least some of the blanks while I tell what I know about the tale."

Mars did as he was instructed, grasping each side of the strange window. He felt it tremble softly – like a grass blade in the wind – Phungi's image vanished while his voice continued to tell the story.

New images flashed across the window as Phungi told how Shroomville came into being. In the window, Mars saw how the first Marshall Shroom – red-haired like him – ran for his life deep in the forest.

He was being tracked by a dark force, a powerful, feral beast that had invaded his forest village, destroying homes and scattering villagers. Strangely, the beast seemed only interested in Marshall Shroom, who used all of his accumulated woodland guile – and not a little of his many forest friendships – to evade the beast's teeth and claws.

Mars watched how his ancestor – that first Shroom looked much like his father, the boy thought – had been hidden for a time by friendly creatures in some kind of underground cavern deep beneath the forest. He couldn't make out what the creatures were because their features were concealed by long cloaks and deeply cowled hoods.

He saw how a dazzlingly white raven came to his ancestor's rescue as the beast darted, snarling with hatred, toward Great-Many Grandfather – standing in the mouth of a cave opening. The raven flew him deep into the forest to set him down well away from the danger.

Mars suddenly understood about some of his own gifts, like how he seemed to be able to communicate with forest creatures like the fireflies, without even having to speak aloud.

He watched as his namesake stumbled into the valley of mushrooms – he called them "living umbrellas" – and saw how they could grow and shape-shift into homes and shops and schools. He understood as Great-Many Grandfather paced out the village borders – exactly as they remained these many generations later – made strange gestures in the air and called out even stranger words. And he watched as the white raven taught Great-Many Grandfather how to summon airborne help when needed.

"Raven, raven from on high;
Come hither when you hear this cry.
When the 'gifted one' summons,
True danger's among us.
Fly quickly when you hear this cry."

And though it seemed to pass in a few instants, young Mars suddenly grasped what all previous first-born

Shrooms had known, as if he had gulped down a large cup overflowing with generations of accumulated knowledge and experience.

He knew now that the strange words and gestures were a spell that hid and protected Shroomville from outsiders – particularly the beast. And Mars saw how his ancestor once more jumped astride the rescuing raven, who returned him to the scattered remains of his former village.

Tears leapt unbidden to Mars' eyes as he watched his forebear round up as many former villagers as he could find. He wept openly as the survivors buried those who had failed to escape the beast's fangs in its quest for that first Marshall Shroom.

The few remaining villagers, one young beauty destined to become Mars' Great-Many Grandmother, gathered up what belongings they could carry and two by two, the raven winged them to the new village-site... and safety.

Shroomville took shape before his eyes, thanks to that first Marshall's wondrous gifts. Mars learned that what outsiders called "mushrooms" were living, breathing plants that shape-shifted for the Constable, whose gift could command them to become homes and shops, libraries and schools.

Generations of images flickered across the magic window. And as Mars soaked up the accumulated lore, he experienced something else.

Mars suddenly felt a hint of the enormous weight of responsibility that rested on his young shoulders.

He also experienced another, more positive, feeling. This time, he knew his father and Portia were alive and that he had to help them.

Just then, the window flickered and Phungi once more materialized before him.

5

The challenge

"Now you understand nearly as much as I," Phungi's shimmering image told Mars. "What we must figure out now is what happened to your father and young Portia Bella. Even more important is to find out why it happened.

"What can you tell me about that, Mars?"

What could Mars tell him about that? After all, just a few hours earlier he was a fairly normal youth, heading to his last day of school before the summer holidays.

What could a 13-year-old tell wise, old Phungi that might help explain the mystery that unfolded today?

"Start by telling me everything that happened to you today," Phungi said. "Spare me the commonplace details of getting washed or brushing your teeth or dressing; concentrate on things that seemed unusual."

Well, thought Mars, there were a few things. So he listed them for the kindly old lore-master:

There was of course the dream about creeping up Hedgehog Hill.

Then there was his mind-drift when he saw the images and heard cries for help from the young friend and the father he missed so terribly. "We want to come home. You have to help us," he repeated, for Phungi.

He told Phungi how his feet – not his head – seemed to take him to Hedgehog after he dropped his books at the trail-fork.

Finally, there was the yellow door that opened of its own accord and the apothecary and the old roll-top desk and... well... Phungi knew the rest after that, so he stopped.

That's when Phinneas T. Phungi filled in some of the blanks.

"You're exactly 13 if I'm not mistaken," the old man observed. "That's the age when first-born Shrooms really begin to experience 'the gift.' It happened that way for your father and for his father before him and for the many first-born Shrooms before that.

"Normally, you would have the luxury of your father teaching you about the gift and how to use it as you grow to maturity. But that was snatched away when your father and young Portia disappeared," he continued.

"And from what you've told me today, it seems that they're still alive and could use your – no, our – help!"

Now Mars loved adventures, the kind he read about in books. But this one was all too real and the prospect of actually living it, sent an involuntary shudder through him.

Then, out of nowhere, something seemed to stop it in mid-shudder and he stood straight and tall before the magic window.

Mars knew there would be danger. He knew too that the danger was not just to him but to his mother, to Phungi and to all Shroomvillagers, if he didn't succeed.

Somehow, without a Constable these past two months, the spell, or presence, or whatever it was that protected Shroomville was weakening.

Somehow, Mars knew the evil force that lured his friend Portia toward Hedgehog Hill, used her as the bait that brought his father to her rescue.

That dark force had drawn Portia to the weakest part of the town's protective boundary and when Marshall Senior stepped out to rescue her, the dark force had them both.

The dark force had started by trying to convince The Constable it was best for the future of Shroomville if he co-operated. But Marshall Senior would have none of that.

Try as he might, the evil one had been unsuccessful in prying the protective spell from him. Two months of trying had been in vain.

However, without a Constable present in Shroomville, one in full possession of the "gift," the spell was weakening and the dark force could sense it. Soon, it would have no further use for Mars' father and young Portia.

Mars suddenly knew the reason for the urgent note in Phungi's voice.

6

Lightening boots and other magic

"I see by your look that our dire straits are revealed to you," said Phungi, gazing intently at Mars, watching the lad's expression change from fear to understanding to a mixture of both. "If we are to succeed, time is of the essence, dear boy.

"If you look closely, you'll see each of the little drawers you first saw as the roll-top rose, are numbered," Phungi continued. "I want you to open a few of them in the exact order I tell you, for that is the order your father gave to me before he disappeared."

On Phungi's instructions, Mars opened a series of drawers, pulling objects from each of them and setting them carefully down on the desk surface. Soon, arrayed before him, were several objects:

- A small rectangular mirror that looked much like the larger talking window
- Supple leather boots, each ankle embossed with a single lightning bolt.
- A shiny, metallic sling, at the end of which was a small, pliable leather cup.

- A pebble-shaped amulet that glowed a soft blue in Mars' hand, returning to opaqueness as he set it down on the desktop.
- A soft leather pouch containing food and water.
- And a short wooden staff, capped at each end with shiny metal orbs.

A strange collection of items, indeed, thought Mars. What in Fern Forest's name were they and how did they work?

But only when he had removed the final object, did the top drawer beneath the desk's surface slowly open to reveal the long-sleeved leather jerkin. It was an exact replica of the one his father donned most days as he left the house to perform his Constable's duties. Whatever they were...

Mars examined the collarless, mid thigh-length garment, fashioned of butter-soft leather that seemed to change colour with the light conditions. He put it on and it fit perfectly, as if a master tailor had measured and sewn it just for him.

Inside, he found pockets shaped to fit each of the objects he'd collected from the desk drawers. Mars quickly stowed them into their proper pockets.

"I know you have many more questions than answers, dear boy," said Phungi. "But time too is our enemy and you must begin your journey immediately.

"Suffice to say that the jerkin itself has powers, as do each of the objects it now holds, but only because you, young Mars, wear it. Some of the objects' powers are self-evident; others will be revealed as your quest unfolds.

"Go now! Take Hedgehog Hill Trail up and away from this old shantytown. That's the direction your father headed when he disappeared and you must follow his steps."

Then, leaning forward and filling the talk-window with his bewhiskered face, old Phungi smiled a smile of gentle reassurance.

"If you need another head to help solve a mystery, use the small talk-window and I'll try to help," he said. "But don't be afraid to follow your own path, even if decisions spring more from the heart than from your already considerable head...

"As for the name over this apothecary, that was my Great-Many Uncle Finbar, who was a close friend of your Great-Many Grandfather," Phungi continued. "Phungis and Shrooms have always been close since then..."

With that, the talk window suddenly went dark and silently slid back into its secret spot, leaving no trace behind it. Mars stood and pushed back the chair as the roll-top too glided silently back into place.

He was left in the pitch-black Pharmacy. Pitch-black until he reached for the amulet – his hand guided to the exact pocket as if he had designed its location. Pulling it out, he noticed that the amulet was now on a leather thong and placing it around his neck, it quickly glowed a blue-white, banishing the gloom and allowing Mars to retrace his steps through the murky darkness.

Stepping past the yellow door, it too snapped back to its slightly ajar position and Mars turned to get his bearings. Though it seemed like only minutes since he first entered the old apothecary, it must have been much longer; the lengthening late-afternoon shadows told Mars he'd best get moving.

Across the town square, he saw the steep path that zigged and zagged its way up Hedgehog Hill. In the late afternoon light, it looked alive with things that slithered, but Mars was sure it was just motes of light playing on gnarled roots and vines that seemed to grow everywhere.

As Mars reached the base of the incline, he learned that it was more than just light that played with his eyes. The gnarled roots and vines seemed alive, waiting to snare him, holding him back from his quest.

He sat on a smooth rock for a moment to think it through when, of its own accord, his hand swiftly reached inside the leather jerkin and retrieved the leather "lightening-bolt" boots.

This was a "heart-hunch" if ever there was one, Mars said to himself. He pulled off his own shoes and pulled on the new boots, noticing that they too fit perfectly, as if a cobbler had crafted them for his feet only.

Strangely, though his old shoes seemed a lot clunkier and were definitely a different shape, they fit perfectly into the pocket from which came the soft leather boots, without causing a bulge. Mars stood and instantly knew the sea of roots and vines that writhed before him would be no obstacle.

As he stepped up the path, a particularly powerful vine snaked toward him from the shadows, aiming to ensnare an ankle. Again, as if his feet had minds of their own, they danced and leapt several feet up the path, hopping Mars deftly out of harm's way.

More vines and roots moved menacingly toward the lad but each time, the boots – almost in a blur of movement – danced him out of their clutches. Soon he had reached the top and the writhing mass seemed to crackle and hiss with fury at missing its prey.

Now, Mars was faced with an even greater challenge. For the top of Hedgehog Hill – a place few Shroomvillagers had ever seen or at least returned from seeing – was actually the edge of a deep and steep abyss whose jagged rock-face disappeared far below into roiling grey mists.

The hissing and crackling grew louder as Mars considered his next move. Then the words came to him:
"Raven, raven from on high;
Come hither when you hear this cry.
When the 'gifted one' summons,
True danger's among us.
Fly quickly when you hear this cry."

Instantly, came the rush of powerful wing-beats and a glistening whiteness alit beside him.

"Climb aboard quickly, young Marshall," said the bird in a soft, clear feminine voice. "I am Windrush and we have precious little time before those roots and vines figure out how you eluded them."

Stepping onto a proffered claw, Mars quickly leapt onto the handsome bird's back, settling between outstretched wings to find a stout leather harness with handles.

The Raven leapt skyward, powerful wings beating, and they shot swiftly out of reach of a crackling noose that streaked out from the shadows.

7

Windrush, the white raven

High into the sky, Windrush soared, Mars holding tight and watching the forest grow smaller beneath him. It was the first time he'd ever been off solid ground and while the flight was exciting, it was also a bit frightening.

Mars gripped the harness ever more tightly... until Windrush asked him to relax his grip or risk hampering the bird's breathing.

"Keep your senses alert, young Mars," Windrush added. "The dark one is everywhere and his minions are many and dangerous."

Just then, Mars' new leather jerkin began to gently vibrate. He knew without asking; it was warning that danger was near.

"Fly swiftly Windrush!" said Mars, over the buffeting of wind. "Someone, or something is pursuing us!"

With that, the great white raven banked steeply to the right, heading for a huge cloud bank just below. Grasping the leather harness firmly, Mars quickly looked above and behind them, just glimpsing an enormous, jet-black, vulture-like winged beast, its wings beating ever faster and swiftly closing the distance between them.

In that short glimpse, Mars also saw the great bird's outstretched talons and hideous, scimitar-shaped beak, on either side of which two bright red eyes glowed evilly. Sitting astride the feathered monster were two black-cloaked figures whose hoods concealed all but the malevolent glare of two more pairs of glowing, fiery red eyes.

"Windrush, bank left… NOW!" Mars shouted.

The white raven, no match in size or speed to its pursuer, wheeled to the left and dropped quickly toward the earth… not a moment too soon as the giant vulture swooped past, missing its prey by inches.

Windrush again resumed his original course, wings beating powerfully as they dove toward the thick cloud bank. Inside its dense whiteness was a measure of safety, Mars realized, for Windrush would blend perfectly. Somehow, he knew that his leather jerkin would also adapt in colour to hide him.

More vibrations from the leather garment alerted Mars to a second airborne attack and he leaned forward to whisper more instructions to his winged friend. Windrush first banked left, then right, then spread his wings to full extension, almost stopping in full hover. The first two moves failed as their pursuer matched them, looming ever closer, but the hover manoeuvre was unanticipated and the flying monster overshot, once again missing its quarry.

This time, however, the cloaked figure threw a container of inky black liquid at them, knowing his prey would attempt to disappear within the cloud and wanting to mark the white bird permanently. Sensing the tactic, Windrush again dodged and wheeled, avoiding the black liquid and this time, slipped into the cloud bank's misty cover.

"That was close, young Mars," said the raven. "Were it not for your sharp eyes and quick wit, I believe we would have perished.

"From now on, speak not aloud, for the Darklings who ride those powerful winged brutes can detect even the faintest of whispers at great distances," Windrush continued, this time sending these words telepathically directly to Marshall's brain. "You can convey your thoughts the same way with me."

"Thanks, Windrush," Mars mind-spoke – wondering how he knew this new skill.

"You're welcome," came the unvoiced reply. "And by the way, you'll soon discover a host of skills you never dreamt of…"

With that, the white raven changed direction, flying swiftly through the thick clouds toward a destination only she knew. There was no time to share this information with her young passenger as Windrush focused all her considerable energies on getting them safely out of harm's way.

Safe for the moment, at least.

As they flew, Mars could only go over his day – the last day of school... his 13th birthday – with some considerable wonder. He reviewed the condensed history of Shroomville provided by the talk-mirror and the information given by old Phungi, his teacher and village lore-keeper.

And then, in all the excitement, he again realized he was flying, something he'd never done before. But now, the fear was gone and, despite the fact he could see nothing beyond the dense mist of the cloud, he began to enjoy the flight.

All food for thought. Thought that raised more questions than answers...

8

An evil uncle

As he rode Windrush the white raven through the almost opaque clouds – having eluded a very determined predator for the time being at least – more questions arose from his eventful day.

Who was the beast, the dark force or the dark one? Why had he captured his father and his friend Portia and was holding them prisoner?

Who, and what, are the Darklings who had attacked him and Windrush?

Who is Windrush and how did she come to know his Great-Many Grandfather? How old is she, given the many generations that passed since the first Marshall Shroom?

And most importantly, what is the extent of his "gift" and where did it come from?

Many more questions began to tumble into that lively, curious mind, but a sudden course change by

Windrush interrupted the lad's thoughts. He clung tightly to the leather harness, leaning into the turn as the white raven tucked wings close and dove sharply left and straight down.

They broke out of the cloud bank at great speed. The sight before Mars made his heart almost leap from his chest. They appeared to be diving directly – and very swiftly – into the top of a thickly canopied forest that would surely mean a disastrous collision.

But this was no ordinary forest, Mars could tell. The leaves that formed what appeared to be an impenetrable canopy were a sickly green colour with patches of scabby brown rust.

An aura of danger... decay... seemed to hover over the vast canopy.

Before Marshall's agile mind could telepathically warn of the danger, they passed through it, unscathed. A round opening in the canopy had appeared an instant before the collision – and just as quickly shut behind them.

"Your gift is strong, young Marshall," the boy heard in his head. "Were I alone, I would have had to wait much longer for the opening and the closing."

Before Mars could even ask himself what he had to do with the opening, Windrush abruptly banked to the left, glided downward beneath the forest canopy and alighted gently on the broad outstretched limb of a massive Oak. Mars took the proffered claw and climbed down onto the wide branch, taking the opportunity to stretch away some of the tension he felt.

Relieving that tension would not be easy, he thought. That aura of danger and stench of decay he sensed earlier was much stronger under the canopy.

Once again, his leather garment vibrated, this time in a way that signalled another presence. Another, not dangerous, presence.

Mars heard them before he saw them, as two huge hummingbirds suddenly appeared, hovering before them, their wings a blur. Brightly coloured, they were small compared to Windrush, but were almost the size of Marshall.

"Do not fear," Windrush telepathed to Mars. "The Hummingbird Nation is an ally and they will report our presence to their people."

At that, the two birds darted off into the shadows and disappeared.

As he sat and changed back to his regular footwear, Windrush turned to face him. "I'm sure you have many questions, not least of which is what is your journey and where do you go from here," she said, telepathically.

"Let me start with some history and then you can ask your questions. I don't promise to have all the answers, but I will try.

"Many generations ago, when your Great-Many Grandfather – the first Marshall Shroom – discovered he had certain powers, saved his people and led them to a new life in Shroomville," the raven began. "As life settled to normal in the little village, he married and soon there came a blessed event."

The event, the birth of the next generation of Shroom, was more important than anyone could have guessed. Because there were twins... born just minutes apart. The elder, of course, was named Marshall and his minutes-younger brother was christened Michael, the raven continued.

Early on in their lives, the boys were very close – almost inseparable. When one would start a sentence, the other would complete it. A craving by one for their mother's succulent, berry-filled bread pudding, was felt almost simultaneously by the other.

"But as they moved closer to that significant age of 13, the milestone you reached today, Marshall, it became clear to the younger Shroom that he would be left behind. It seemed just unfair at first, when Michael's minutes-older brother began to exhibit some of his gifts. And as time passed, that feeling festered."

There was a 13th birthday party for the twins and that's when Marshall Senior spoke privately and at length to his elder son, explaining the gifts he inherited as first-born and starting the instruction he would need to use them wisely. But he also took young Michael aside, explaining that as the younger sibling, he inherited some gifts, but his elder brother was destined to become Shroomville's village constable.

"That's when the seed of unfairness really rooted and began to grow into full-blown jealousy," said Windrush. "From then on, the two brothers slowly grew apart; and while they were identical twins, it soon became dead easy to tell them apart."

A smiling face, intelligent, pale blue eyes and sunny disposition quickly identified Marshall. As for Michael, an almost permanent scowl seemed to be his constant companion.

Michael also took to disappearing for hours at a time. No one knew where he went and he would always return, a little more withdrawn than before. It was as if he had a secret known only to him.

"Well, as it turned out, Michael did have a secret," Windrush went on. "As it turned out, Michael had been using his minor powers to sneak free of Shroomville's and Hedgehog's protective dome. That's where, just before he reached his 16th birthday, Michael encountered the soothing, worm-like tongue of the feral beast – disguised as a playful otter, to appear less threatening. Still strong, was his ambition to bring your people under his power, despite being thwarted by your Great-Many Grandfather."

"Why haven't I heard any of this before?" Mars blurted telepathically.

"Patience, young Marshall," Windrush soothed. "If your father had not been abducted, he'd be the one telling you this story right now. It's one that had to await your 13th birthday."

With that, the raven continued her story. Michael's absences grew longer, until one day, he disappeared up the exact same Hedgehog Hill trail Mars had taken earlier that day. He never returned.

Search parties came up empty and those who lived in what became the shantytown began to feel nervous about living close to what seemed to be the edge of evil. Soon, they abandoned their homes and shops and trekked back into Shroomville.

Many generations passed without incident until The Beast once more renewed his goal of taking over Shroomville. His great powers allowed him to continue grooming Michael, who also took on considerable dark powers, one of which was virtual immortality.

Over that time, Michael also took on a new name. He became 'Maliset, The Dark One.' And his evil powers grew very strong.

"About a year ago, using his knowledge of Shroomville's protective dome and his own dark powers, Maliset drew up a plan to take advantage of your friend Portia's fondness for exploration and mind-planted a powerful suggestion that lured her to Hedgehog Hill," Windrush continued. "And when your friend's natural curiosity brought her there, Maliset abducted her, knowing that the Town Constable would soon follow the trail in search of the missing girl.

"Sure enough, your father tracked Portia to the edge of the chasm where we met today. "Right there, was a gap in Shroomville's protective dome. It was enough for

Maliset and his evil followers to surround and capture your father.

"They carried him off to Maliset's lair, deep in Murkwood forest and they've been working on him since then to find how to break down Shroomville's defences and bring your people under his dominion. Their malicious efforts to break your father's spirit have so far been unsuccessful: but they have taken their toll.

"A few days ago, I detected his and Portia's combined telepathic cries for help – a message that was intended for you, Marshall. I knew you had not yet reached the age of 13, which meant your "gifts" were not yet fully bestowed.   But I also sensed that you had begun to realize you were somehow different than your peers.

"So on your 13th birthday, I added my own powers to boost your father's telepathic 'signal.' That's when we reached you, and you know the rest..."

9

Murkwood Forest

Mars sat in silence, his mind trying to grapple with Windrush's startling story... wondering what was next... hoping that his father and Portia were still alive and safe. Many questions remain, he thought, and moments later, they leapt from his mind like the staccato tapping of a Woodpecker's bill on a tree.

"Then where are my father and Portia now and are they safe?

"How am I supposed to help them?

"What chance do I have against Maliset, who's been perfecting his dark powers since my Great-Many Grandfather's time?

"And by the way, how old are you; how could you have known my Great-Many Grandfather?"

Though difficult to describe exactly, the raven's features seemed to soften as she held up a wing to stop the torrent of questions.

"There is no time to tell you much more, Marshall. It is now up to you, your heart, your intuition and your gifts.

"Tonight, just before dawn but while darkness prevails, I will take you close to Maliset's lair," came the raven's thoughts directly to Marshall's mind. "Meanwhile, if you search your new leather garment, you'll find food and drink to help fortify you on your journey.

"After that, you must rest, restore your strength, calm your restless mind and prepare yourself for what lies ahead."

At the mention of food, Mars realized he hadn't eaten for several hours. He was suddenly famished and quickly found that inside pocket; his hand returned again and again with nuts, berries, a stout Shroomville hard-tack and a small skin of water that seemed never to empty, no matter how often he quenched his thirst.

His hunger satisfied and the remaining provisions re-stowed in the pocket, an overwhelming fatigue came over the lad and he fell fast asleep, a watchful Windrush at his side.

Which is when the dream began...

"I knew you'd come, my son," said the familiar voice of his father. "And not a moment too soon, for these past two months have been exhausting. I know I wasn't there to prepare you for your 'gifts,' but you must use them soon if Portia and I – and indeed, Shroomville – are ever to escape the clutches of Maliset."

The voice of his father continued for some time as he slept. They stopped with these words:
"Be wary of Maliset for his dark powers are considerable," his father's voice continued. "He was able to strip me of many of my gifts when he captured me. He senses you have some powers but also senses the weakness of inexperience and will try to exploit that. Your gifts alone will not win the day, my son. But if you follow your heart

and that strong intuitive sense that I had begun to see in you, victory can be ours... yours, mine, Portia's and all of Shroomville's. Our collective future is at stake."

With that, another voice interrupted and he felt his shoulder being shaken as Windrush woke him gently from his deep sleep. It seemed like he'd drifted into sleep only moments ago, but he awoke refreshed – overjoyed to know his father was alive and had spoken to him.

Most importantly, he awoke with the strong feeling that if he kept his wits about him, together, they just might pull it off. That too, he traced back to the dream...

"We must fly quickly now, Marshall, for dawn approaches," the raven told the lad's mind. "What little I know about Maliset's lair I will pass on to you.

"Remember, communicate with your thoughts only. Now climb aboard."

Marshall climbed onto the raven's back and grasped the leather harness firmly as Windrush leapt aloft with powerful wing-beats. All around him was blacker than his own basement in the dead of night – that is, before he met and helped the fireflies...

As dark as it was, Windrush flew unerringly, deftly swerving through the dense forest. En route, she also passed on what she knew – and what she didn't – about Maliset's lair.

Occasionally, Mars glimpsed patches of inky blue sky, dotted with uncountable stars, and pictured his grieving mother – wondering what she was thinking under that same sky. He wished he could somehow tell her that he was safe... for now!

He wished he could comfort her... hug her.

"If wishes were barleycorns," he said ruefully to himself as they flew through the inky darkness. "I'd have a sack-full."

Finally, the raven touched down on a tree limb high above the forest's brush-covered floor. After closely examining the area all around their position, Windrush stepped away from the limb and silently glided down to a small clearing.

"That path before you will lead to the lair," she instructed. "Be swift, Marshall, for I must depart."

Marshall leapt off the raven's back, alighting silently on the forest floor. Just as quickly, he reached for the lightening-embossed leather shoes, which he promptly drew over his feet, stowing his regular boots back into the accommodating pocket.

At the same time, Windrush leapt stealthily into the air, but before she disappeared into the gloom, she transmitted a final thought message.

"Remember your father's instructions in your dream as you slept tonight," she admonished. "In particular, remember to heed your heart and obey your intuition. Those are strengths that Maliset could not have prepared for."

Moments later, Windrush was gone, leaving Marshall to hastily check that all was stowed properly in the leather jerkin's inside pockets. He knew he would need every item. That's when he felt the vibration. Reaching inside the jerkin, he removed the small talk window, taking care to keep it concealed.

This time, two figures shimmered into focus. Mars was looking directly at old Phungi and his mother.

"I was so worried about you, Marshall," his mother said. "So I asked old Phungi if he could contact you.

"He's filled me in on what you're doing and I wanted to wish you luck," she whispered.

Pointing the talk-mirror down, Mars quickly dried the tears that began to form and then looked straight into his mother's face.

"I know there's danger here, but I can't just leave Dad and Portia in the clutches of Maliset. Try not to worry, Mom; soon we'll all be together."

With that, he returned the talk mirror to its pocket.

He then turned and plunged quickly and sure-footedly down the path before him. Making not a sound, the extraordinary footwear – he now called them "lightening boots" – bore him swiftly onward for several minutes down a path that was little more than a zigzag of barely detectable ruts in the earth.

The self-doubt of youth continued to gnaw at him. He wondered again how he could possibly succeed against Maliset, whose generations of honing dark powers vastly outdid his one day of experience.

As he sprinted down the crooked path, Mars drew strength from his parents' – and Windrush's – words and arrived at one inescapable conclusion.

He knew he must try…

10

Maliset confronted

As the extraordinary lightening boots deftly steered him along the twisty path, Marshall suddenly felt that familiar pulsing of his leather tunic – alerting him to approaching danger. Quickly, silently, he came to a halt behind a copse of thick undergrowth and carefully parted some branches to peer beyond.

Before him lay a clearing and an astonishingly large mushroom-shaped structure. Astonishing, because this mushroom seemed to be constructed of stone, revealed in places where its smooth covering seemed to have cracked and fallen away.

Almost spanning its broad centre stem was a stout oak door, arched at the top and braced with riveted metal reinforcing bands at its edges and criss-crossing the width and height of its centre-opening halves.

There were no windows at "stem" level but above on the cap and to each side of the door were two narrow, oval-shaped windows that gleamed wickedly red – like huge, malevolent eyes – in the pre-dawn darkness. A circle of windows that ringed the very crown of the mushroom-shaped structure was barely visible.

It was Maliset's lair and it seemed unguarded – at least on the outside – Marshall's senses told him. Though there was no way to confirm it, Marshall also sensed his father and Portia were imprisoned somewhere inside the evil-looking structure.

Something told him to change back into his regular boots; he did so, silently returning the lightening-boots to their inside pocket.

Creeping quietly into the clearing, he focused on the stout portal and wondered how to get inside, when one half of it silently swung open... just like the yellow door in the shantytown. Making no sound, he slipped past the opening and the door shut softly behind him.

Inside, he crept up several steps, emerged into the main hall and peered into the gloom. All was dark except for a shimmering reddish glow from bright coals in a giant stone hearth. As his eyes became accustomed to the murkiness, Marshall took in a vast, circular, domed hall that seemed oddly larger than the external dimensions of the structure could possibly allow.

There, to one side of the hearth, stood a stout wooden cage and through its slats, Marshall could make out the vague outlines of a table, two chairs and, wait, what appeared to be two sleeping figures.

He crept closer, swivelling his head constantly to ensure no one else was in the hall.

"It's them!" Marshall thought to himself as he approached the cage's well secured door. "I've found them!"

Just then, the figures stirred, arose and Marshall found himself staring wide-eyed into the faces of his father and Portia. Placing index finger over his lips to signal silence, the lad reached through the bars to touch them.

Father and son embraced, then parted to let Portia into the hug. Then came the familiar quivering of his leather jerkin.

"This is all too simple," a now alarmed Marshall Junior thought to himself.

It was. Suddenly, torches on a huge wheel suspended above them flared into life, banishing the gloom.

"How touching," boomed a deep voice, dripping with disdain. "Shroomville's village constable and his son, finally reunited.

"I didn't foresee how easy it would be to lure you here, young Marshall."

More torchlight flared, illuminating a raised throne directly across the circular hall as the trio spun to face who was speaking.

But while they refocused across the room, something more menacing occurred. The stout cage's door instantly opened and the jail expanded, engulfing Mars with Portia and his father, its door slamming shut with a heavy click.

More torches flared, lighting their new predicament. Remembering the warning not to tip off Maliset to his powers, Mars decided not to try and mind-open the re-locked cage.

Movement from across the circular room suddenly refocused the trio's attention. As Mars peered beyond his prison, a lone figure – with a disturbingly familiar gait and appearance – strode confidently toward the caged trio.

Following, a few paces behind in menacing semi-circle formation were eight diminutive Darklings, red eyes burning beneath cowls and claw-like hands protruding from their cloaks. Mars shivered.

Evil – and the acrid stench of decay – radiated from the entourage like heat from a bonfire. He'd never sensed anything so strongly.

"How perfect," said the oddly familiar figure as he approached. "It's like a family reunion."

Now the figure came to a halt, standing brazenly in front of the cage. More torches flared to life and the figure tore his own hood back to reveal his face.

"Criminy!" thought Mars. "How can it be?

"This man could almost be my father's twin!"

An eerie resemblance at first glance, yes. But anyone could easily tell the two apart. On closer inspection, the strange figure standing outside the cage bore other features that quickly set him apart from The Constable.

First, but for traces of greasy grey hair at the fringes, he was completely bald, his smooth pate revealing multicoloured, tattooed runes and other symbols that seemed to radiate an aura of dark magic.

Bristly white eyebrows formed jagged peaks over coal black eyes. Below a bony, hawk-like nose, a thin-lipped mouth full of crooked teeth sneered back at them.

Nothing friendly about that face, Mars thought to himself.

"Allow me to formally introduce myself, young Mars, though I'm sure you have figured out who I am," said the thin, icy voice, dripping with sarcasm. "I am Maliset, your – I'm sure – beloved Great-Many Uncle."

In the increasingly bright room, Mars suddenly noticed some other details that surprised and shocked him. Details that opened another door to despair…

11

Captured

Staring intently at Maliset, Mars could see how closely he resembled his own father. He could also see how different they were.

He wondered if Maliset's thready, greasy grey hair – if it was allowed to grow back – would be flaming red like his father's. That's when he turned to gaze on his father and was shocked to see some deep changes there as well.

What was once a head of thick, somewhat unruly red hair was now peppered with grey. Those kindly eyes – piercing blue and filled with wit and wisdom – were now a paler blue. It was as if a light had been turned down behind them.

His father's face was now a rabbit warren of lines and creases, his brow more heavily furrowed. Slightly stooped, as though carrying a great weight on his shoulders, his father's eyes now looked almost directly into Mars'.

"He looks exhausted," thought Mars. "He's struggling to stay awake... to stay in control."

"I am exhausted, son," said a voice inside his head. "But now you're here, the two of us may be a match for Maliset. Remember, any important communication between us must be mind-to-mind from now on. Though once he might have – before he embraced evil – Maliset can no longer read our minds. But we need to keep up the pretence that our only form of communication is verbal."

Maliset's eyes snapped quickly between Mars and his father. He suspected something was passing between father and son but ruled it out. "My powers far exceed theirs," he told himself.

"Father, what has he done to you," Mars blurted aloud for Maliset's sake.

Mars then swerved his gaze to Portia. She too looked tired but her eyes signalled the same intelligence... the same strength... and her lips formed a ghost of a knowing smile. An instant later, Mars was astonished to hear her voice in his head.

"Your father was able to teach me some basic telepathy skills when we were first captured," she explained, looking away so Maliset would not suspect they were mind-speaking. "We speak aloud to make Maliset think that's our only way to converse. And when we do, we never reveal our true thoughts."

Then, out loud, she turned to him and said: "Oh Mars, I never thought I'd see you again. But we're so tired, let's try to talk tomorrow."

Mars turned and looked accusingly at Maliset.

Then, taking his cue, Mars turned back to his father: "You look exhausted, Father. Why don't you lie down for awhile.'

"And Portia, I can tell you too can hardly stay awake. We'll catch up later after you've both slept."

"Come, Portia," his father replied, eyes swollen and shoulders sagging with exhaustion. And with that, the weary pair moved deeper into the cage, where they lay down on sleeping mats.

Maliset, however, did not move, continuing to gaze intently into Mars' eyes. It couldn't be they're mind-speaking, he thought to himself. The boy is too young and has not received his father's instructions. And Portia is not part of the family.

Stepping back a pace, Maliset looked his young captive up and down, suddenly noticing the boy's butter-soft, pale brown leather jerkin.

"What have we here," the captor asked scornfully. "Perhaps you'd like to show us what you carry inside that leather garment."

Mars' heart sank. If Maliset discovered the pockets, he'd confiscate their contents. And being without those gifts from old Phungi would make it very difficult to escape.

Very difficult, indeed.

That's when he felt a barely noticeable shuffling movement inside the jerkin. And he instantly knew he could show Maliset the inside of the garment.

"This is a gift from my mother," he said, playing at a cringing cower before his evil uncle. "It's nothing special."

"Nevertheless," said Maliset. "You'll humour me, won't you? Show me the inside... Now!"

Again, retreating a half-pace, as if in fear, Mars reluctantly grasped and held open both sides of the garment as Maliset stared intently at it. Inside, the leather was as smooth as the outside; no pockets or other openings were visible.

"Move closer!" he barked. "I want to check it for myself."

Again, Mars complied... slowly... timidly... holding the garment open with shaking hands. As the boy approached, Maliset reached past the bars with both hands, pulled Mars' face roughly into the cage. Then, he scrunched each side of the garment with one hand to ensure it held no surprises.

The garment gave no hint of its secret contents. Maliset stepped back, satisfied that the young Constable-to-be was just not in his league.

"We'll continue this in the morning," he snarled. "But I warn you, my patience wears thin. If you don't give me what I want, I don't know what might happen to your father…

"Or Portia for that matter," he added, with lip-curling menace.

There was no missing the implication in that statement, Mars thought.

"So why have you brought us here?" Mars asked, timidly. "Why did you abduct my father and my friend?"

"Your father knows and I think even you, young Mars, may have begun to grasp why as well," came the reply. "I've suffered as the ignored, lesser younger brother for too long.

"Finally, I'm ready to assume my rightful place in Shroomville. Finally, Shroomville will be mine… to rule as I please!"

Mars' heart sank. Worry lines creased his young brow.

That's when the leather jerkin again began to quiver. Not in a way that anyone beside the wearer would – or could notice – but almost imperceptibly. Only this time, the warning was not of danger, but rather opportunity.

This time, it told Mars something different… or at least confirmed one of his intuitive leaps.

"Great-Many Uncle or not," Mars thought, knowing his father could hear this mind speak. "Maliset is not as confident as he puts on. He's got some doubts and we need to play on them if we're to escape."

"Tomorrow, one of you will tell me what I need to know," Maliset declared, eyes casting back and forth between Mars and his now-prone father – finally settling on Portia. "I don't think either of you would want anything to happen to Portia."

"You'll never succeed," Mars blurted, his voice cracking with feigned bravado.

"We'll see," said Maliset, a cruel grin curling his lips. "We'll see…

"But perhaps you need some time to think over the tight spot you're in. "We'll try to make you as comfortable as possible, but I can't guarantee it'll match life in Shroomville."

With that, Maliset spun and strode quickly away, black cloak billowing behind him like a dark cloud. Overhead, torches dimmed as he passed them. Finally, surrounded by his Darklings, he disappeared into an opening beside his throne, leaving the huge chamber in near blackness.

Mars knew he had only a few short hours to prepare for Maliset's grilling.

With a sinking feeling, he turned and strode into the cage toward the reclining figures of his father and Portia.

12

Preparing for interrogation

"What do we do now?" Mars despaired, watching Maliset and his fawning followers disappear. He turned again, peering out into the gloom, then retreated deeper into the cage-prison and lay down on a mat beside his prone fellow prisoners.

"I agree, son. Maliset is not as confident as he'd like us to believe. Together, we may have a solution," came his father's mind-speak voice. "It just hasn't occurred to us yet."

Feeling suddenly exhausted, Mars agreed, closed his eyes and motioned to the others to do the same. "Let's sleep on it."

For a short time, before pretend sleep was overcome by the real thing, Mars, his father and Portia telepathically continued to discuss the events that led to their capture. It was then Mars was finally convinced that Maliset could not "hear" the trio's mind-speak conversations.

"Of course!" the youth thought. "You originally contacted me telepathically. If Maliset had intercepted that message, my thoughts would have been open to him and I would have been captured at the cliff above Hedgehog Hill.

"And as soon as I started to mind-speak with Windrush, Maliset's Darklings were flying blind. It's as if we're on a different thought-wave. Maliset can't hear our thoughts."

"That's right," his father and Portia agreed in unison. "That may be our best advantage."

"It may be our only advantage," his father added. "Now… sleep; we'll need to be at our best tomorrow."

Mars lay back on the sleeping mat. "That may not be our only advantage," he thought to himself as, this time, the leather jerkin pulsed softly and rhythmically, dropping him almost instantly into a deep slumber.   Portia too, fell quickly asleep… but not Mars' father.

Slowly, silently, he manoeuvred himself so his head lightly touched his son's and he began a ritual as old as Shroomville. It was a ritual known only to Town Constables and their first-born sons.

In the hours that followed, while Mars slept peacefully, the Constable shared his powers and his knowledge about Shroomville.

"Mars will need everything I can give him if he's to withstand Maliset's interrogation tomorrow," the Constable thought to himself, as he too, finally succumbed to sleep.

13
The interrogation

It seemed only moments after dropping off to sleep that Mars awoke – still surrounded by the inky-blackness of Maliset's lair. He could make out the outlines of his father and Portia and could hear their soft, regular breathing.

Soon it will be dawn and the next meeting with Maliset, Mars thought, steeling himself for what promised to be an unpleasant encounter. Suddenly, one of the leather garment's inner pockets pulsed softly... and then more forcefully.

Moving furtively to escape notice by any who might be monitoring the trio, Mars reached directly into the pocket and pulled out first a soft skin containing water and second, a Shroomville hard-tack. A particular favourite, Mars recalled fondly how his mother mixed the densely packed flour, lard and milk, kneaded the mixture over and over and then formed round biscuits for the oven. Packed with nuts, raisins and fruit peel; a heavy, tea biscuit-sized portion was a day's nutrition.

"If we're to stand up to Maliset today, we'd better make sure we have the energy for it," Mars thought. He then furtively nudged his father and Portia, quickly cautioning them telepathically to make no sound or movement.

Mars then explained his never-ending supply of food and water, reached in and found portions for each of them. All three remained under the scrubby blankets provided them as they ate and drank silently. Mars then retrieved the water container they shared and stowed it back in the proper pocket.

"I see you've paid a visit to the desk-of-many-drawers at the old Phungi Apothecary," his father observed telepathically. "What else have you brought...?"

But before Mars could respond, a shaft of daylight shot past the ledge of the high windows that ringed the chamber piercing the murky blackness. A column of hooded Darklings – eyes glowing blood-red in the receding gloom – marched toward them.

As they surrounded the cage, Maliset's now familiar voice – dripping with venom – penetrated the early-morning gloom as he seemed to magically materialize before them.

"I trust you've slept well," came his mocking morning greeting, "And I presume that you've come to the logical conclusion that resisting me is futility itself. Because if you haven't, I'm more than willing to demonstrate my powers. And some of them can be very uncomfortable indeed."

"Ask me what you must, Maliset," Mars replied. "But I warn you, I know very little about what you speak.

"But before we start, I'd like some food for me and my companions..."

The words were barely out of Mars' mouth when Maliset erupted into cackling laughter.

"You are in no position to make any demands, young Marshall Shroom," said Maliset as he regained his composure. "And as for what you know, perhaps your discomfort will prompt your father to volunteer the information I need."

With that, Maliset gestured with one hand and backed away from the cage, whose door suddenly swung open. Two Darklings quickly grabbed Mars, bound his hands behind him and dragged him, struggling, before their master, who was now seated atop his throne. A long, dark metallic staff glistened malevolently as he balanced it across his knees with one hand.

With the other hand, he again gestured and torches lit magically throughout the large chamber, their flickering light seeming to concentrate in a circle around Maliset and Mars.

This is not good, Mars thought to himself. With my hands bound, I have no access to the pockets and no way to use any of my gifts.

"Is the great Maliset so fearful of a 13-year-old that he insists on binding his hands," Mars taunted his evil Great-Many Uncle. "Surely your own powers and your strutting Darklings are more than a match for me."

And, with a furtive glance to his father and Portia, he mind-spoke to them: "Do not – under any circumstances – volunteer any information to Maliset, no matter how 'uncomfortable' I appear to be. Believe me, much of what you witness will be play-acting for Maliset's benefit."

That's when the interrogation began. It started with innocuous queries such as how old was Mars, what level of schooling he had attained and what was his favourite colour. Where the response didn't seem important, Mars gave a one- or two-word truthful reply and fell silent, awaiting the next question.

"So, you turned 13 without the benefit of your father being at your side," Maliset offered. "What a pity. Your father had much to teach you…"

Minutes stretched into hours and as the questions became more pointed, Maliset became increasingly agitated at his captive's uncooperative responses.

"How did you know your father and Portia were still alive," Maliset growled.

"I've always felt they were alive but somehow lost," came the response.

"Surely you don't expect me to believe there was no communication between you and your father," Maliset broke in. "No one leaves Shroomville's protective dome on a whim… on a foolish expedition into the dangers of the outside world."

"Believe what you wish," said Mars. "I know nothing about what you call the 'Shroomville dome' or 'the dangers of the outside world.' All I know is my father and Portia disappeared outside of the shantytown and I went there to try and find them."

"Then how did you get past my trapping vines and how did you summon Windrush, the White Raven?" Maliset roared.

"What vines? I just ran around them. And as for Windrush, how would I know how to summon her? She was just there at the top of the cliff."

"You lie, young Marshall," Maliset thundered, pointing the metallic rod directly at him. "Perhaps you should experience the price of your lies."

With that, Maliset's features morphed into a gargoyle-like mask of fury and a red crackling bolt shot from the staff directly at Mars.

Mars could feel the leather jerkin begin to pulsate violently even before the rod erupted with its charge. The garment seemed to shrink ever so slightly around him, continuing to vibrate.

Expecting great pain as the bolt struck him, Mars was surprised to feel very little discomfort. It was as if the leather jerkin's vibrations cleverly matched those of the charge, but exactly out of phase, cancelling it out.

But Mars also knew he could not reveal the garment's powers. Shaking violently, he shrieked in feigned terror and pain before his cruelly smiling captor.

Maliset raised the staff, pointing it over Mars' head. As the bolt of energy ceased, Mars fell to the ground, faking a dead faint.

"He's just a boy, Maliset," cried out Mars' father. "He's no match for you. Why don't you question me instead?"

"Do not fear, Constable, your turn will come again. And perhaps we'll test young Portia in the bargain, to see what she knows."

After a gesture from Maliset, the Darklings roughly picked Mars up and brought him to a kneeling position. Still pretending injury, and with arms still bound Mars swayed to and fro, shaking in feigned fear.

Another bolt of red lightening shot from Maliset's staff. Once again, the leather jerkin warded off the worst of the pain and the boy again crumpled like a rag doll into pretended unconsciousness.

The Darklings once more surrounded Mars, pulling him roughly to his knees before Maliset.

"Unbind his hands so he can keep himself erect before me," Maliset ordered. "I want to look into his eyes as I question this young deceiver. I also want his father to see the price of his son's deceit."

The Darklings untied Mars' hands and the lad propped himself up on hands and knees, weaving back and forth before his captor. Again, he pitched to one side, this time throwing a furtive glance back to his fellow captives.

"Don't volunteer anything, Father," he mind-spoke to them. "The leather garment is affording considerable protection. I can hold out for now."

"Tell me how the protective dome works," Maliset ordered, again lowering the staff to point at Mars. "Tell me!"

"I know nothing of a protective dome," the lad replied.

With that, Maliset's face once more contorted in rage, and the lance erupted, striking Mars with its crackling energy. As before, the leather garment vibrated to block the bolt's impact, and again, Mars seemed to writhe in agony until Maliset lifted the lance.

Mars pitched to one side and 'fainted' before his tormentor.

"Enough!" cried Marshall Senior. "Can't you see he can't help you? And even if he could, he certainly can't respond when he's unconscious."

"You may have a point, Town Constable," Maliset replied. "I grow weary of your son's duplicity. Perhaps a night of reflection – and the prospects of my questioning young Portia – might loosen his tongue.

With a contemptuous gesture, Maliset rose and stalked out of the chamber while the Darklings dragged young Mars and threw him back into the cage, its door clanging shut behind them.

"Enjoy your short respite, young Marshall," he tossed over his shoulder. "I promise you, it won't be as restful as your first night…"

14

The torture continues

"I do know the information Maliset wants," Mars thought as he continued feigning unconsciousness. "But how?"

"I gave it to you last night," came his father's voice. "While you slept, I shared some of my knowledge – and my powers – to help you withstand Maliset's torture.

"You are the next Town Constable, Mars. When we return home, I will resume as Town Constable... but only for the time it takes to instruct you in how to use these powers... When you are ready, the powers that keep our town safe from its enemies will ultimately reside in you alone."

Shifting slightly, Mars risked a squinted-eye look at his father. It was a risk that nearly proved his undoing, for in the murky light of the chamber, Mars saw that his father had changed dramatically and he had to use all his strength to remain still in the eyes of his captors.

There before him, his father had aged overnight. Even more lines and wrinkles criss-crossed his face and the luxuriant full head of red hair – which had only just begun to show flecks of grey the night before – was now white as snow.

If his father's dramatically aged appearance wasn't enough to make the young man react, what followed surely was.

Suddenly, the chamber exploded with ear-splitting chants and thunderous, staccato drum beats, punctuated with piercing screams. At the same time, all torches leapt into tiny suns of light, turning the chamber dizzyingly bright.

The three captives convulsed, clapping hands over ears and clenching their eyes shut against the piercing light.

"Cover yourself with the blankets as if to protect yourselves against the blinding light," Mars transmitted to his father and Portia. "And try to keep moving in time with the noise while I find a way to block it."

Still convulsing, the trio drew the tattered blankets over them and Mars reached into the protective garment; six small strips of leather fell magically into his hand.

"Form these into a wad and put them into your ears so they can't be seen by the Darklings," Mars instructed telepathically, slipping the leather strips to Portia and his father. "They'll make the noise manageable while we plan how to get out of here."

Reaching back into the jerkin, Mars once more found the nourishing hard-tack and water, passing portions to his fellow captors as they continued to writhe in play-acted pain.

The food and drink revived their spirits and restored their strength somewhat, enabling Mars and his father to continue 'reacting' to the cacophony and bright lights. But Portia could not maintain the ruse; she was just too exhausted.

Alarmed, Mars feared his captives would discover their ploy and without thinking, he passed a hand over her face and muttered an incantation he'd never heard himself speak. Portia fell immediately into a deep sleep, though her body continued to twitch in time with the clamour.

To the Darklings, who watched them attentively, the rest of the long night appeared to be pure misery for their captives. Now and again, Mars or his father would abruptly leap to their feet, grasp the bars of their cage and scream for the noise to stop and the bright lights to dim, only to slump to the floor clutching ears and hiding under blankets.

The ruse worked.

Behind the cacophony and dizzyingly bright lights, the pair was hatching an escape plan. Mars telepathically shared with his father details of the items concealed within his leather jerkin. And as daylight shot shafts of light through the overhead windows, the torches abruptly dimmed and the clamour ceased – but just for a moment – reminding them how silence truly can be golden.

15

The plan unfolds

Silence reigned… at least for the moment.

Mars took the opportunity to stealthily lift the spell he'd placed over Portia and her eyes fluttered open. He then furtively collected the leather strips and returned them to an inside pocket, just as he heard movement from the area around Maliset's throne.

"I trust you slept well," Maliset's now familiar reedy voice pierced through the din. "Now it's time for you to tell me what I need to know."

Shoulders slumped in defeat, Mars and his father turned exhausted faces toward Maliset, while an obviously terrified Portia cowered and shivered in fear behind them.

"All right Maliset, you've won," said Marshal Senior, pulling himself wearily to his feet and shielding his eyes against the again-intensifying light.

"We'll talk. But you've got to lower these lights and stop the noise. And we want out of this tiny cage for awhile… just to walk around and clear our heads.

"You can see that we're in no shape to fight you. And your Darklings have us greatly outnumbered."

"You're in no position to make demands," Maliset glowered back at him.

"Perhaps not," the Constable replied, "but our requests are small ones. Trust me, they'll help."

"All right," said Maliset, nodding to his Darklings and motioning with one hand. At that, the torches extinguished themselves one by one. With another, almost imperceptible twitch of one, cruelly arched eyebrow, the stout gate locking them in swung open silently.

Still feigning exhaustion, Mars, his father and Portia shuffled out of the cage and into the huge chamber. Surrounded by a horde of hooded Darklings – their eyes glowing like red-hot coals – Mars and his father stretched and twisted to bring circulation back to their weary frames.

"My patience wears thin, young Marshall," Maliset announced. "Don't take advantage of my generous nature."

Portia continued to cower in fear behind them as the pair stretched, when suddenly – with a shriek – she dropped to the floor, convulsing in pain.

Leaping to her side, Mars and his father dropped to their knees on either side of Portia. With all the confusion, the Darklings' circle began to close, but no one noticed Mars reach furtively into his leather jerkin and then don the lightening boots.

Seconds later, he rose to his feet and leapt right over top of the advancing Darklings.

"Seize him!" Maliset shrieked.

The Darklings began to close, but Mars easily evaded them, thanks to the magic of the lightening boots.

"Now, Father!" Mars shouted. Reaching into an inside pocket, Mars extracted what appeared to be a round, leather-covered stick and tossed it expertly to his father. Catching the instrument deftly, Marshall Senior muttered a low incantation.

Instantly, the stick lengthened to staff length, gold-coloured metal orbs emerging from each end. Circling quickly and expertly spinning the staff, the Constable waded in to the small circle of Darklings. With lightening quick blows, he dispatched one, then two and finally six of the menacing Darklings, their bodies slumped into unconsciousness.

Across the Chamber, Mars continued to deftly evade more advancing Darklings, spinning and twisting, leaping and gyrating away from their gnarled talon-like hands. He reached once more into the jerkin, this time for his own weapon.

Out came the sling, its supple metallic cord swinging ever faster over his head – adding an ominous keening sound to the increasing mayhem. The Darklings reversed their advance, cowering backwards.

Watching with dismay, Maliset gestured toward the magic cage, hoping to once more enclose his captives. But Mars and his father both anticipated the move.

Turning their attention to the expanding cage, the two Shrooms focused their minds on it in a battle of wills. Suddenly, the cage began to retract.

Maliset's face, contorted with fury, soon washed with surprise... and then alarm. Focusing more intently on his captives, the cage again began to expand, snaking menacingly toward the elder Constable and Portia.

Once more, the two Marshalls turned their considerable attention to the magic cage, its door swinging open and shut like a monster's jaw. Again, the cage hesitated, then shrank until with a loud metallic snap, its door shattered into pieces.

His sling swinging ever faster over his head, Mars turned his full attention to an astonished Maliset. With a gesture, he loosed the sling's projectile, which shot across the chamber almost too fast to see with the naked eye.

Mars' aim was true. The perfectly round heavy stone struck Maliset squarely on the forehead, dropping him like a sack of potatoes.

16

They meet new allies

Tucking the sling quickly back into its pocket, Mars surveyed the chaos. Maliset lay stunned and moaning in pain beside his throne. The now leaderless Darklings cowered in the shadows awaiting instructions.

"Quickly," Mars telepathed. "Let's move. Maliset won't be out forever."

Shortening his staff so it could easily be wielded with one hand, Marshall Senior scooped up Portia over his shoulder and swiftly followed his son toward the huge oak door.

As before, Mars merely "thought" it open and they dashed through it. Outside, Mars halted for a moment, commanded the door shut and this time, locked it with a stout wooden bar.

Together, Marshall junior and senior recited the now familiar words to summon Windrush.

"Raven, raven from on high;
Come hither when you hear this cry.
When the 'gifted one' summons,
True danger's among us.
Fly quickly when you hear this cry."

This time, however, Marshall Senior added two words: "Bring Help!"

Moments later, a powerful thrumming of wings could be heard and Windrush alighted. Gesturing to Marshall Senior and Portia, they quickly climbed aboard and Windrush leapt into the air.

More powerful wing-beats. Suddenly, a coal-black raven landed beside Mars.

"I am Java, young Mars," the raven telepathed. "Quickly, we must fly. There will be pursuers."

Leaping aboard Java's back, Mars gripped the leather harness and the raven flew off into the gathering dawn.

As Java and his passenger lifted off, Mars heard pounding below. It was the sound of someone trying to break down the stout oak door.

"Quickly," Mars told the ravens telepathically. "We must put some distance between us and Maliset's forces. That locked door won't slow them for long."

Their precious cargo clinging to leather harnesses, the two ravens redoubled their efforts, flying swiftly through the forest. The trees rushed past in a blur for their passengers as Windrush and Java deftly navigated around them, slowly gaining altitude.

"Keep a sharp eye all around us," Windrush transmitted. "Maliset can summon his dark forces from far and wide and he has many eyes and ears in this evil forest.

Seconds later, Mars saw the evidence of Windrush's warning. From the ground far below, more of the vines he first saw at Hedghog Hill were racing up the broad trees toward them.

Suddenly, the air below them roiled with the vines, snaking swiftly toward them as the ravens put all they had into gaining altitude.

Onward and upward they flew, Mars and his father keeping watch in all directions. As they approached Murkwood Forest's dense canopy, Mars once again gestured with his hand and a perfectly round hole suddenly appeared and just as quickly, closed behind them.

The ravens and their passengers were now winging west above the forest, which slowly transformed beneath them into rolling meadows as they headed toward a range of mountains in the near distance. With the still-low sun behind them, Mars watched their two shadows follow the grassy contours below.

That's when Mars' leather jerkin began to vibrate with ever-greater urgency. Another shadow – and the sound of other, more powerful wing-beats – gave away their pursuers.

"We have company," Mars transmitted. "They're probably five minutes behind us now, but gaining fast."

With those words, the two ravens banked and dove toward a river valley that wound lazily through the open meadows toward a cut in the nearby mountain range.

Looking up Mars and his father were alarmed to see the largest net imaginable descending rapidly over them. Worse yet, above the net the sky was black with vultures and their hooded, flaming-eyed passengers.

There seemed to be no escape.

17

The moles

Mars and his father, however, had other ideas and they were quickly communicated to Windrush and Java as they dove at a dizzying speed toward the river valley. Seconds before impact, the two ravens – one behind the other – pulled up and banked left toward a nearby rock face.

Once again, just before contact, Mars concentrated on the rock face while his father focused upward, slowing the huge net's descent. With the full power of the young man's increasingly agile mind focused on it, the rock face opened like a giant iris.

The ravens and their passengers shot through the opening just before the giant net would have snared them and, just as quickly, the opening closed with a metallic "snik" behind them.

Mars quickly reached inside the leather jerkin, pulled out the pebble-shaped light amulet. Holding it over his head, the amulet cast its bright bluish-white light, illuminating a cavernous chamber. The two ravens quickly landed and their passengers dismounted.

"Thank you, young Mars; that was too close for comfort," Windrush transmitted. "Your gifts – and your intuitive powers – continue to grow quickly."

Out of nowhere, a ring of torches blazed into life, enabling Mars to tuck his light amulet back into its pocket. High above them, Mars thought he saw movement on a ledge that ringed the cavern. Turning his attention to the torches, he willed them to burn even more brightly and again scanned the ridge.

Small figures – their eyes glowing a soft green in the flickering shadows scurried back out of sight into crevices in the rock. As Mars reached inside his leather garment for a defensive weapon, he was stopped by Windrush.

"Do not worry, they are friends," the Raven said, this time aloud. "They can help us escape from Maliset and his evil legions."

As Mars returned his hand to his side, one of the creatures leapt agilely from ledge to ledge, landing lightly before him. Standing a bit more than shoulder high to Mars, its eyes looked up and met the lad's own – in a gaze that was intelligent, friendly... and unafraid.

Clad from head to toe in a black cowl tied at the waist, the creature lowered its hood to reveal a rounded, tapering muzzle not quite hiding a pair of white, chisel-sharp teeth and revealing intense green eyes under grey-flecked eyebrows and small pointed ears. Mars could see the creature's velvety brown coat had turned grey at the chest.

Perched atop his snout, rimless spectacles accented those intelligent eyes and reflected an aura of age and wisdom. Hands and feet were broad and strong – and equipped with razor-sharp claws.

"This is Digg-ar, leader of the Mountain Moles," said Mars' father, with a slight bow toward the creature. "This is their domain."

"My ancestors well knew the first Marshall Shroom – your great-many grandfather," Digg-ar continued. "There is no time to relate the tale now; it is enough to say that we have helped each other during other, very dangerous times and for generations, we have vowed to continue our alliance."

Windrush jumped back in – this time telepathically.

"Mountain Mole leaders can understand us telepathically, thanks to the original Marshall Shroom passing on this gift," he explained. "We stand in their domain. Few are as adept beneath the earth as Mountain Moles.

"We're safe... for the moment," the raven continued. "But rest assured, Maliset is even now working his considerable powers to enter here.

"We must flee. Digg-ar and his people will help us evade Maliset and his evil army."

With a signal from the Mole leader, several more of the creatures appeared, distributing black cloaks to their visitors. As the ravens and their three passengers donned the cloaks, Digg-ar explained that they would serve as both camouflage and as protection against subterranean chill.

Soon, the company – a torch-wielding Digg-ar in the lead – moved swiftly to the far end of the huge chamber.

Three tunnels abruptly appeared out of the shadows.

18

Beneath the earth

Standing before the three tunnels, Mars halted the troop.

"From now on, we communicate only mind-to-mind," he transmitted. "Maliset cannot detect it but if we speak aloud or make other noises, his extremely sharp-eared Darklings will hear."

With almost inaudible clicks, Digg-ar passed on these instructions to his people. Followed by Mars, his father, Portia and the two cloaked ravens – a dozen of his subjects bringing up the rear – Digg-ar headed directly into the middle tunnel. Rounding the first gentle curve, Mars heard scraping noises and stopped quickly.

"What is that? Has Maliset broken through already?"

"Be calm, Master Shroom," Digg-ar transmitted. "My people are sealing this tunnel so even if Maliset does get there, he'll not detect it. Soon, my people will split up and start down the other two tunnels; I've instructed them to make the odd noise that evil ears will detect."

"I get it," the lad replied. "That'll force Maliset to split his own forces. But what'll happen if the Darklings catch your people?"

"My people are resourceful and not without their own wiles, young Mars. Remember, this is our realm and we have survived – and thrived – for generations beyond memory."

Onward they trekked, maintaining absolute silence. The tunnel twisted and turned, alternately heading up and down, seemingly following a route of least geographic resistance.

"This tunnel would make a snake dizzy," Mars thought to himself.

Just then, Digg-ar's torch sputtered out, leaving the group in total blackness but for the eerie pale green of the mole men's eyes.

"I feared this might happen," Digg-ar mind-muttered. "We can see quite clearly in the blackness but I'm afraid our new friends cannot."

"Don't worry," Mars replied. And reaching into a secret pocket inside his leather garment, he withdrew the amulet. "I think this will help."

With that, Mars fixed the amulet into a small pocket that opened on his right shoulder and willed it to burn brightly. Soon the tunnel was ablaze with blue-white light and the assembled group continued.

They moved onward, maintaining silence along the circuitous route for another hour when suddenly Mars sensed a change in the air. It seemed cooler, less dank.

Moments later, the amulet's blazing light dimmed of its own accord and he detected a dim light far off down the tunnel.

"Time to extinguish completely that remarkable light, young Mars," Digg-ar transmitted. "We'll move very slowly and very carefully from here on.

"At my signal, stop and make not a sound."

Moments later, Digg-ar's arm shot up in the lessening gloom, halting the procession. Making eye contact with one of his men and nodding quickly, the scout moved quickly and silently down the tunnel into the gloom.

Moments later, the scout returned and huddled with Digg-ar, discussing his findings in a series of soft, almost inaudible clicks that Mars could not decipher.

"Mixed news, I fear," Digg-ar translated. "My scout could see nothing at the tunnel entrance. But like all Mole-men, his senses are highly attuned and I particularly trust this scout's intuitive insight.

"He sensed a malevolence – plus hints of an intent to disguise its presence – in that part of the valley where we had planned to emerge, and fears it could be a trap. We'll need to adapt our plan somewhat."

With that, came another click-tongue conference. Shortly, the two grasped shoulders, touched foreheads and the scout and six of his followers scurried forward to quietly seal up the small peep-hole.

Then came more soft scraping noises, which slowly waned until Mars and his companions could hear nothing.

As if to answer an unasked question, Digg-ar explained that the scouting party was digging a new tunnel, this time under the valley. And since the new passageway was through the valley's lush, peaty earth, the tunnelling would go quickly… and quietly.

"Be patient, my friends," Digg-ar transmitted. "My people will soon return and we will proceed."

With that, Mars once more retrieved and illuminated the amulet. And from another secret pocket, he withdrew water and hard-tack for all.

"We should rest now," Mars telepathed, as he lay down on the soft earth. "We will need clear minds and all our strength, if we are to outwit this enemy."

Mars and his companions soon slipped into slumber.

Digg-ar waited a few moments, until he was sure Mars slept, before he too carefully lay down, aligning himself so his head gently touched the lad's temple.

"Enough to communicate directly but not enough to wake the lad," was Digg-ar's last thought before he too fell into an exhausted sleep.

19

Dangerous Detour

Mars awakened with a start to a click-talk conference between Digg-ar and the now-returned scouting party. Digg-ar stopped and turned to face Mars.

"We move out now," Digg-ar transmitted. "Night will soon fall in the valley.

"A caution, my new friends," he continued. "Because speed is of the essence, our escape tunnel is quite narrow. We all will have to bend low in places to negotiate it.

"But do not fear; the detour is not long…"

With that, the party moved into the tunnel, Mars, his father and Portia scrunching down to hands and knees in places. The two ravens tucked wings and legs close to their bodies, crouched their necks and stepped a bit awkwardly into the narrow opening.

On they crept through the channel as it wove its way left and right, up and down through the rich, loamy earth of the valley. In places, the tunnel dipped precipitously and Mars and his friends literally slid head first down a steep slope.

His magic amulet glowing once again, Mars followed Digg-ar as the tunnel's downward slope began to level out. The party veered left, then right, then straight.

Though he heard not a hint of complaint, Mars sensed a mounting discomfort from Portia and his father. If it was anything like his own – hands and knees raw and back screaming with pain – Mars silently praised them.

Not much farther now, young Mars," Digg-ar mind-whispered. And presently, the party emerged into a hastily dug larger cavern where they could stand nearly erect. There, awaiting their arrival, was Digg-ar's chief scout who welcomed his leader in their soft clicking tongue.

"What have you found, my son?" Digg-ar asked the scout.

"Day has turned to night, father," came the clicking reply. "And we have a narrow escape window… before the full moon takes away our long-shadow advantage."

Mars followed the exchange when he suddenly realized, "I can understand their language! How come I couldn't before?"

Digg-ar stopped and turned to the lad. "Yes, my young friend. While you slept, I used a trick your Great-many Grandfather taught my forebears and passed on to you our language and knowledge of the terrain between here and Shroomville."

Digg-ar was right, Mars quickly realized. He knew exactly where he was and what the valley looked like outside.

He also knew how dangerous was their plight but how – with speed, courage and ingenuity – they just might make it. Turning to his father and Portia, he quickly shared his plan telepathically, finishing with an admonition he had often heard from his father but never thought he would make…

"We won't have much time," he said. "Follow my instructions to the letter. The Darklings have gathered in considerable strength; they are Maliset's eyes, ears and muscle.

"We must be quick, observant, stealthy."

Mars turned to Digg-ar and, grasping the old one's shoulders, leaned forward and gently touched foreheads. It was the traditional Mole-man act of deep gratitude and respect that Mars intuitively adopted.

"Time flies, my friends," Digg-ar clicked, so his followers could understand. "Before we start, please know better my chief scout, Burr-oh. He is also my son and heir. And before this adventure ends, I'm certain you will meet again."

Mars and Burr-oh quickly grasped shoulders and touched foreheads – as did Marshall Senior and Digg-ar. Instantly, they were fast friends… enlisted in the same battle against Maliset and his evil.

The final, most dangerous element of the battle was about to begin.

20

Battle in Wisteria Grove Valley

Burr-oh turned to Mars and his companions and mind-spoke: "We all know the plan and how much it depends on exact timing and lightening quick response. Let's move out now!"

With that, the party turned abruptly and silently emerged into the cool early evening air, thoroughly hidden inside a huge, thick grove of wisteria, interwoven with sweetly scented lilac bushes.

Mars quickly shed his mole-cloak and took the lead of his party, guiding his father, Portia and the two ravens unerringly along what seemed to them, an invisible path.

It twisted and turned past gnarled roots and high, straight shafts that entwined and knit themselves into an impenetrable wall of wood and leaves. From the outside, the grove was a crescendo of pale, lavender blooms and green leaves.

Inside, it was a living tunnel.

Digg-ar, Burr-oh and their men quickly disappeared into the gloom in another direction. As the groups separated, Digg-ar mind-spoke to Mars… "Remember, my young friend, when you hear our diversion, you know what to do. Act quickly!"

Nodding, Mars picked up the pace, his companions scrambling to keep up, and the party raced silently through the interior of the dense grove. Soon, they came to a parting of the dense bushes. Mars held up his hand and, touching index finger to lips, once again cautioned them to maintain silence.

"We have only seconds, Mars mind-spoke to them. "When you hear the diversion, Windrush, you and Java cast off your cloaks, go out first and be ready to fly!"

Without warning, cries of alarm from the hooded and cloaked Darklings – accompanied by thumping sounds of a series of cave-ins and frantic scratching – penetrated the dark evening.

"Go! Now!" Mars transmitted.

Quickly shedding their cloaks, the two ravens scrambled out into a grassy meadow and spread their cramped wings.

"Climb aboard Java and hold tightly to the leather harness," Mars instructed his father and Portia. "Windrush and I are right behind you."

Java leapt into the air, Windrush moments behind, and with sturdy wing-beats they soared higher and higher over the valley. As they gained altitude, Mars shot a quick look down at the scene below.

It was chaos... at least for the Darklings. For where each of them had hidden, waiting to spring their own trap, was a shallow, narrow hole and a hooded figure struggling to get out.

Digg-ar's forces had tunnelled beneath and, at their leader's signal, quickly opened a trap beneath their enemies.

"Brilliant," thought Mars. "They dug the tunnels exactly the right depth so when the Darklings dropped, their arms were pinned."

Suddenly, Mars' leather garment began to vibrate... starting on his left shoulder-top, to be exact. The victory on the ground was evidently short-lived, the lad thought to himself.

As the magic garment pulsated ever more fiercely, Mars grabbed firmly onto the harness with both hands – one on either side of Windrush's muscular shoulders – instructing his father to do the same with Java and to follow his lead.

Like guiding a toboggan downhill in winter – and taking his cue for danger's location from where his leather garment juddered and quivered most – Mars leaned quickly to the right. Windrush in the lead, the two ravens banked right. Then, following Mars' intuitive guidance, the birds picked up the pace, veering left, then right, then up in a dizzying series of manoeuvres.

High into the air, they soared. Suddenly, Mars' leather garment began to throb all over. Danger was coming at them from virtually every direction... except one.

"Down! Now!" the lad mind-spoke, and abruptly the two birds tucked wings close and dove like falling arrows toward the earth.

Faster and faster, the two ravens dove, Mars in the lead aboard Windrush, guiding her with deft weight shifts. Looking over his shoulder, Mars quickly saw the source of the leather garment's vibrations; at least six huge vultures – each ridden by a hooded Darkling – were swooping ever closer.

Another quick glance back and Mars could also see the Darklings, red eyes flashing malevolently deep in their cowls, readying a huge weighted net to drop on them.

More subtle weight shifts and the two birds levelled out somewhat, feinted left – then right – then resumed the dive. Behind them, the manoeuvres worked, causing the Darklings to delay dropping the huge net.

"This is it," Mars telepathed his companions. "On my mark, execute the next part of the plan!"

21

The Wysteria-Lilac Nation

"Three... two... one... NOW!" Mars transmitted.

With that signal, Windrush banked hard to the left... and Java pitched hard to the right. As expected, the Darkling posse split evenly, with three vultures chasing each of the ravens.

Moments later, the two ravens quickly swung back toward each other, flying side by side at great speed just as another long, thickly canopied Wisteria-Lilac grove came into sight. The Darklings struggled to keep their quarry in sight as Windrush and Java picked up speed, heading straight for the grove.

Though less able to manoeuvre, the Darklings' vultures were larger and more powerful. Soon they were gaining on their quarry.

At Mars' signal, Windrush and Java each dove straight down toward the grove's lavender canopy which opened and closed like an iris, swallowing the airborne Shroomvillagers.

Inside, the ravens slowed their breakneck speed, taking care to brush leaves and branches, making noise for the Darklings to hear and chart their whereabouts. Again, as predicted, the pursuing Darklings reined back the vultures, slowing their forward momentum.

Ahead in the leafy green canopy, unbeknownst to the Darklings or their airborne steeds, the Grove was subtly changing. Strong, supple Wisteria tendrils snaked from the grove's canopy, entwining their narrow girths with each other for even greater strength.

In the still moonless gloom, the Darklings levelled out just over the canopy, concentrating so hard to hear their quarry's position they failed to detect the living lassos that coiled furtively in the lavender canopy just beneath them.

Clicks of alarm from the Darklings and coarse squawks from their vultures shattered the moonless night. Three of them were quickly snared and because of their speed, were held fast and dashed to the rocky ground beside the groves. Vultures and Darklings lay senseless.

Grasping the danger, the other three Darklings quickly gained altitude to escape the roiling vine-trap, which shot higher to keep them at bay.

Meanwhile, inside the groves' thick foliage, a reunion took place. As Windrush landed, Mars alighted to once more grasp shoulders with Digg-ar. Just behind, Java and her passengers were greeted by Burr-oh.

"These groves are more than just beautiful foliage," Mars observed as he touched foreheads with Digg-ar.

"As I said earlier, young Marshall, we Mole-men have our own resources," Digg-ar replied telepathically. "For generations, our people have been allied with the Wisteria-Lilac Nation.

"According to our lore, one of my ancestors kept this intelligent species alive at a time of drought by bringing it water from deep inside our mountain home. Since then, we have grown ever closer – especially when it comes to keeping Maliset and his minions at bay."

"Something happened to at least some of the Darklings after we entered the grove," said Mars, "and I'm sure I heard a familiar tongue."

"Your senses grow ever keener, my young friend," Digg-ar replied. "There is little time for the full story now; but the Darklings were once part of my people... until Maliset lured them away with evil promises of dominion over all.

"We fought – and defeated – an attempted coup, stripped the mutinous ones of their Mole-men powers and cast them out of the mountain.

"Since then, of course, they have served Maliset above ground. He has given them different, dark, powers and those vultures to ride."

Outside, the three remaining vultures could be heard circling overhead just out of reach of the now-snapping Wisteria tendrils. Raising his hand to capture their attention, Burr-oh signalled silence and led Java and her two passengers around Windrush, Digg-ar and Mars.

"This is where we split up," Mars mind-spoke to his father and Portia, hugging each warmly as they followed their guide. "Stay with Burr-oh and he will lead you past this danger and show you the path back to Shroomville."

"Be careful, Mars," his father and Portia said in unison as they crept quietly forward behind Burr-oh.

"I don't like leaving you alone to face Maliset, but your plan holds the best prospect of safety for Portia and success for you," his father added, as he disappeared into the gloom.

Steering the Constable and Portia deftly through the gnarled trunk-branches of the grove, Burr-oh stopped quickly as a hole in the earth quietly opened up before them. Soft, almost imperceptible clicking emerged from within, along with the heads of two hooded mole-men.

"Follow me," Burr-oh told his charges, the group quickly dropped into a newly dug tunnel beneath the grove. No sooner were they out of sight than the grove knit itself over to hide the passage.

"I'm grateful for your help, Digg-ar," Mars told his companion. "I don't wish to put you in any further danger, my friend. So please feel free to rejoin your people."

"Ah, that cannot be, young Marshall, for this battle has been foretold," came the reply. "Maliset grows ever stronger and over time, there is little doubt that alone, we could not continue to withstand his power.

"But together, according to our teachings, there is a chance to defeat this evil. Together, our efforts could mean the sun will once again penetrate into Murkwood.

"Stay with the plan. The risk is well worth the potential defeat of Maliset."

Mars nodded in agreement, his respect for Digg-ar and his people growing. Quickly, the pair climbed aboard Windrush to resume their quest.

22

Through the Darkness

In pitch blackness beneath the dense Lilac-Wisteria grove, Burr-oh led his charges unerringly through the narrow, winding tunnel. At first, the passage descended gently, then veered ever-so-slightly left... then right. On the way, the travellers passed several other tunnel openings leading in different directions.

As the tunnel straightened, Burr-oh and two of his fellow mole-men stopped to light small torches. With the new illumination, the group was able to make faster time.

"Be very careful and maintain absolute silence," Burr-oh mind-spoke to his charges. "The Darklings' hearing – like ours – is very acute."

With that, the crew crept along the passage as quickly as it could go without scraping the tunnel walls – or floor.

After nearly an hour, Burr-oh's scout abruptly held up a hand and the company once more halted. Not far before them, Marshall Senior could see where the passage ended.

"This is where we continue above ground," Marshall telepathed to Portia and Java. Grasping Burr-oh by the shoulders in the Mole-men's tradition of friendship, the Constable leaned forward to gently touch foreheads.

"I cannot thank you enough for your counsel… for your help," the Constable told his friend. "Please also pass on to your esteemed father – and all your people – my deep gratitude. We are forever in your debt."

"It is our debt to the Shroom family that is now repaid," Burr-oh replied. "If our battle with Maliset is successful, I am sure we shall meet again.

"You know the way from here, Constable. But I caution you, remain vigilant; Maliset is very powerful and his eyes and ears are everywhere."

With that parting advice, the Mole-man reached quickly inside his cloak and handed the Constable a soft leather shoulder bag bearing a wide strap. Slipping the strap over his shoulder, Marshall signalled Portia and Java to follow him.

Carefully, Burr-oh's scout opened a passage outside and the three figures quietly climbed up and through, emerging inside yet another Lilac-Wisteria grove.

"Where are we?" Portia telepathed. "How far are we from Shroomville?"

"Fear not, little one," said Java. "Now that we're above ground, my senses can once again detect the earth's forces and as soon as I can see the stars, I'll know even better. We are not far from your home, but we must proceed with extreme caution."

With Java temporarily in the lead, the trio moved silently forward. With no light source, progress was slow.

Soon, they detected a slight breeze and saw its source, an opening in the grove wall. Soft starlight poured a pale light across their path as the trio once more stopped.

Moving into the lead once more and instructing Java and Portia to remain where they were, the Constable crept carefully toward the opening. Reaching into the soft leather knapsack, he silently removed a stout, though short, staff and grasped it with both hands.

Suddenly, the constable froze as a shadow – a cloaked and cowled Darkling, he reckoned – passed across the starlit opening.

Portia's heart sank as she too recognized the shadow's familiar outline. "Constable," she mind-spoke. "Do you also know the Mole language?"

"Quick thinking, young lady," he replied, instantly grasping her plan. "Now, not a sound, you two."

Creeping close to the opening, the Constable could now plainly see the clearing and its lone occupant, pacing back and forth on watch. Blood-red eyes sweeping to and fro, the Darkling was nothing, if not thorough.

No doubt remained. The Constable leaned forward slightly, emitting a series of soft, staccato clicking sounds. The Darkling halted in his tracks, swivelling quickly toward the opening.

More clicks from the Constable... this time with more urgency... more authority. The Darkling stiffened, bowed, clicked back and moved smartly beyond the bushes to the edge of the clearing.

Moments later, the cloaked Darkling reappeared, this time leading a vulture. Swiftly, he harnessed the huge bird, tied it securely to a stout Lilac-Wisteria branch and moved toward the leafy opening to stand at attention to one side.

Now, Portia and Java could feel an ever-so-slight vibration from the grove, followed by a soft rustling sound as if the Lilac-Wisteria too, were following orders. Slender tendrils intertwined and softly crept at ground level – kept out of sight by grass cover – toward the Darkling and his flying steed.

But the Darkling's own keen hearing also detected the warning rustle and, though surprised, he quickly moved to untie the vulture, preparing to clamber aboard and escape.

The Constable leapt from the shadowed opening, both hands grasping the staff, which instantly tripled in length.

Again surprised, the Darkling turned to face his assailant, slowing his advance toward the vulture. The pause was just enough for the Constable to plant his feet and club the cowled figure senseless... before the Darkling could click a warning to his companions.

At the attack on its cloaked master, the vulture tried mightily to stand, but was tethered fast by its harness.

Clumsily, the raptor tried to shift its weight to engage one razor-taloned claw to slice the tether.

It was too late. Strong, slender tendrils leapt from the shadows and twined around the bird's claws, holding them tight.

More tendrils snaked unerringly up one side of the vulture, wrapping around the great bird's neck... tightening to ensure not even a faint warning croak escaped its cruelly curved beak. With both legs secured and a overwhelmingly tight grip around its neck, the vulture's eyes rolled inward as it slipped into unconsciousness, rolling over onto its side.

Quickly, more tendrils wrapped its now-closed beak as others ensnared and gagged the Darkling, ensuring it too, would not soon escape or sound a warning.

At the Constable's signal, Java jumped into the open, spreading his wings and beckoning to Portia to climb aboard his muscled shoulders. After satisfying himself that the Darkling and his flying steed were indeed secured, the Constable silently thanked the Lilac-Wisteria for its help and jumped up behind Portia.

The black raven leapt skyward and with powerful wing-beats was quickly airborne, heading low and south in the gloomy predawn sky.

At the same time, Windrush and her riders flew swiftly in exactly the opposite direction...

23

The battle looms

High above the open meadows, Windrush flew swiftly back toward Murkwood Forest, so far undetected by the Darklings, who had blindly followed the false trail left by Mars and Digg-ar.

This time following Digg-ar's directions, the white raven flew directly to the mountain where her charges had first met the Mole-people and their leader.

As before, Windrush flew at top speed directly at the sheer vertical cliff where, just before there would have been certain collision, an entrance opened and shut swiftly behind them.

Deftly alighting inside the vast, dimly lit cavern, Windrush and her two riders were quickly surrounded by what seemed to be uncountable Mole-people – each clutching a stout wooden staff, at the end of which gleamed a metal spear-point.

Gesturing for Mars to follow, Digg-ar scrambled up a nearby outcropping so the pair stood solemnly before a sea of grey cloaks and bristling spears.

"My people," Digg-ar clicked. "Tonight we face a perilous battle against our longtime foe, Maliset and our former brothers who the evil one corrupted." Digg-ar turned slightly, grasped Mars by the shoulder... and continued.

"Tonight, I am confident we will be victorious – thanks to a brilliant plan devised by our friend Marshall Shroom!" Clicked cheers erupted spontaneously.

"While we helped the Constable and Portia return to Shroomville, you were all briefed on the plan and have begun to position our forces.

"We are ready... as ready as ever. And with the help of our friend Mars, I believe we have a better than even chance to make sure the sun once more penetrates Murkwood Forest."

With that, Digg-ar and Mars climbed back down and, with Windrush, moved quickly toward the middle of three broad tunnels that loomed before them. Behind them, the Mole-men split into three columns, some of them following Digg-ar and the rest scuttling into the other two passages.

As before, when the main forces had disappeared, a few Mole-people remained behind to seal up all traces of the tunnels, even to the point of brushing the cavern floor to eliminate footprints.

"What am I doing," Mars asked himself as he ran down the centre passage. "Less than a week ago, I was home in Shroomville, heading for the last day of school with a knapsack full of books.

"Now look at me! I'm armed. I have a head-full of new knowledge and a sea of new friends.

"And I'm scared nearly witless!"

His thoughts turned abruptly to his mother and father... and to Portia, his classmates... even to Mrs. Crimini, old Phungi and to all Shroomvillagers. Although probably only old Phungi – and perhaps his mother – realized it, they were all counting on him for their very existence.

If Mars and his new allies failed, it wouldn't be long before Maliset spread his evil dominion over Shroomville. It wouldn't be long before sunlight and fresh air would become strangers to his village.

"I can't let that happen," Mars muttered softly as new strength... fresh determination surged through him.

Though he could hear none of Mars' thoughts, (the lad had ways to keep his own counsel when necessary), Digg-ar kept glimpsing the boy's expression as they rushed headlong down the tunnel.

But he did detect Mar's muttered final vow and quickly determined that the lad had been second-guessing himself but in the final analysis, had steeled himself for the upcoming battle.

Stopping the band for a moment, Digg-ar took his young friend aside locked eyes with him.

With hands on Mars' shoulders, Digg-ar's features softened. A ghost of a smile spread across the old mole's face as he mind-spoke to the young man.

"Do not fear, young Mars. You have already proven your courage – and your intelligence – when you rescued your father and Portia and escaped Maliset's clutches.

"You now also possess your father's considerable knowledge, some of mine and you have an army of allies you didn't have before. I believe there's a very good chance that your father and Portia are already safe in Shroomville."

Sensing the young lad wanted to reply, Digg-ar held up one clawed finger and continued. "Just listen, for now, my young friend.

"Best of all, you have learned to trust a great heart that is backed by considerable wisdom for one so young. And it has served you – and Shroomville – well over the past few days.

"They will serve you well for this final battle."

Squaring his shoulders, Mars stood taller. A new look of resolute determination claimed the lad's face.

"Thank you, my friend," Mars telepathed, leaning close to touch foreheads. "This entire journey and the battle we face would have been impossible without your considerable help.

"Before we proceed, I have something to attend to," said Mars, moving away from his ally. Reaching into an inside pocket of the leather jerkin, he pulled out the smaller 'talk-window' and held it firmly with both hands.

Almost instantly, an image materialized and he telepathed an update of his situation to old Phungi back in Shroomville.

"Be prepared," he mind-spoke to the old teacher. "My father and Portia are en route and should arrive in Shroomville very soon."

"Do not worry, young Mars," Phungi replied. "I will watch and listen for them."

With that, Mars replaced the talk-window in its pocket and returned to Digg-ar's side. Together, they rejoined Windrush at the head of the Mole-company and resumed the march.

Before long, the Mole-company encountered two of Digg-ar's scouts and once again halted. Following a short clicking update by the scouts, Mars and Digg-ar turned to face each other, brows furrowing with new resolve.

The final battle was at hand.

24

The Constable and Portia

Far to the south, well away from Murkwood, Java and his two passengers flew swiftly onward in the gloomy predawn, keeping a wary watch for any pursuers.

The Constable felt it first, but Portia soon turned to lock eyes with her friend's father. Java was losing altitude and their course was drifting regularly and almost imperceptibly to the east. The raven was favouring his left wing.

"Take us down, Java!" the Constable ordered telepathically. "Land quickly!"

Thinking the Constable had detected danger, Java banked steeply, spread his coal-black wings and descended silently, landing – uncharacteristically – with a hop that nearly spilled his riders onto the rocky ground.

"Sorry for the rough landing, my friends," Java apologized.

"No need to be sorry," the Constable replied. "We can see that you're injured."

"I had hoped to get us to Shroomville," said the raven. "But I fear I have injured one wing and strained its muscles during those furious manoeuvres earlier. I must rest and heal before we continue."

Marshall Senior and Portia moved quickly to the raven's side, helping him toward a nearby thicket of low, thickly canopied shrubs. Beside it, a stream burbled a meandering path across the mostly open land.

Gently, but firmly, the Constable examined Cloud's left wing, confirming their worst fears. The valiant raven was indeed, badly injured.

"We will be walking the last leg of our journey," he mind-spoke to the bird. "You are in no condition to carry us further."

At the sound of rummaging beside him, the Constable turned to see Portia frantically searching her pockets. Breaking into a smile, she found what she was looking for and withdrew a small, familiar object.

It was the amulet from Mars' leather jerkin… the one that helped light their way through pitch-black tunnels to freedom. This time, however, it glowed a deep, barely visible orange in the girl's hand as she proudly displayed it.

"Mars and I have been close friends… nearly all our lives," she telepathed, addressing Java directly. "A year or so ago, I was chasing him through Fern Forest near our homes when he tripped and fell into a nearly dry creek-bed."

The result, she continued, was a torn pant-leg and a bleeding, badly gashed shin – almost right to the bone. Sitting him down beside the stream and rolling up the pant-leg, Portia gently scooped water over the wound, tying a ripped-off corner of her own shirt tail around it to stop the bleeding.

"I thought I'd have to leave Mars and go for help," she told them. "But as I tended the wound, we were both amazed to see the bleeding stop and the wound start to scab over."

It was as if the girl's own hands had helped quicken the healing. A few minutes later, the pair scrambled to their feet and ran home, as if nothing had happened. In the way children often do, Portia had quickly forgotten the amazing incident… until now.

"What does that have to do with the amulet," Java and the Constable asked in unison.

"When we split up, Mars passed me the amulet and reminded me of my healing skills," she replied. "He told me that they would be much enhanced using this amulet."

Moving to Java's injured wing, the amulet softly glowing in her hand, Portia parted the raven's feathers and gently ran the smooth stone back and forth across the damaged muscles. With this contact, the amulet began to grow warm and vibrate rhythmically. Its soft light also changed… to an almost blinding orange-yellow light – shafts of which splayed out here and there through the raven's black plumage.

The Constable arose quickly and covered the procedure with his thick cloak.

But not quickly enough. Not before an errant, bright yellow light shaft caught the eye of a Darkling, watching from atop his vulture, high in the northern sky above the plain.

Obeying his rider's clicked command, the feathered monster banked steeply and streaked toward the light source, which had quickly winked out as the sun began its daily sojourn across the sky.

The vulture's strong approaching wing-beats alerted first Java and then the Constable and Portia. The amulet safely stowed, the trio huddled together closely, keeping the leafy thicket between them and the approaching vulture.

Closer and closer, the vulture swooped, its carrion-claws clacking in the wind… its red-eyed rider scanning for the light source. Just then, a slim arc of sun scattered countless rays of orange dawn through gaps in the eastern sky's thin band of cloud cover.

One of those rays directly struck the meandering stream, reflecting instantly upward and abruptly blinking out as the cloud cover thickened to block it.

"Just some reflected morning sun," the Darkling clicked, banking the vulture to the right and guiding it once again higher and northward. As the rising sun bathed the earth with its warmth, the Darkling and his flying steed soon disappeared over the northern horizon.

Java stood and flexed his wings as the Constable carefully scanned the skies and their surroundings. No one was in sight.

"Remarkable!" Java telepathed. "That torn muscle is like new! Quickly, climb aboard; we must fly!"

His two charges aboard, Java was soon airborne but staying close to the earth to take advantage of the long shadows of early morning. A narrow band of dark cloud on the eastern horizon helped them by delaying a full-blown sunrise.

High above, stars winked out in a sky that slowly transformed from indigo to deep azure to pale blue.

Looking up, Portia saw it first... two narrow, white tracks snaked straight as an arrow across the sky behind what appeared to be a strikingly silver, fast-moving bird.

"What is that?" she mind-spoke to her companions. "I've never seen anything like it before."

"We have," the constable and Java telepathed back in unison.

"I can shed little knowledge of what it is, except to say it comes from far away and flies very high... much higher than we can," said Java. "And occasionally, I can barely hear the powerful roar it emits... as if it were some kind of volcano."

"But I don't sense any evil in it," the Constable added, "so put it out of your mind, Portia."

They flew on in silence through the gathering dawn.

Though they had flown a considerable distance, it seemed like only minutes when the trio looked down on a welcome sight. Straight ahead of them loomed Hedgehog Hill, where both Portia and the Constable had been abducted.

"Some of Maliset's evil still clings to this place," the Constable mind-spoke. "Let's avoid it; fly to the west until you see 'The three Sentinels.'"

"O-o-h yes," Portia chimed in. "Those tall trees stand shoulder-to-shoulder, like lookouts guarding Shroomville. And they're a short walk from the village."

Following the new flight plan, Java veered east and quickly spotted the Sentinels. Swooping low to scan the area, the raven landed gently at the foot of the three towering conifers, their broad, ground-level girth shielding them from the village.

They were home!

The Constable and Portia leapt quickly to the forest floor, moving close to hug their black feathered friend.

"That was some flying, Java," said the Constable, this time aloud now that the trio were within Shroomville's protective dome.

"Thank you," Java replied, bowing gracefully and turning to Portia. "And a special thanks for your healing hands, young lady.

"Now, I must fly, for I detect that my mother Windrush may need my services."

"Be safe, Java," called the Constable, as the raven took to the sky. "Remember, whenever you or Windrush wish to visit, signal us first and we will meet you here, so as not to upset our villagers with any sudden avian appearances."

As Java disappeared beyond the trees, the Constable knew he had one more duty to perform. He sat Portia down and after a short talk, they slowly climbed the path that gently rose to their village.

Home.

25

The final battle

Standing shoulder to shoulder, Mars and Digg-ar rallied the Mole-people to battle.

Following a single gesture from Digg-ar, the caped and cowled army of Mole-men rushed past the pair, leaving one trusted scout behind. As the company disappeared around the next tunnel bend, Digg-ar and Mars turned and this time, pressed their foreheads against the tunnel wall.

"Launch now!" they click-telepathed in unison, transmitting the order through solid earth to the rest of the Mole commanders. Moments later, they detected confirming responses that the order had been received and understood.

The final battle had begun!

Mars, Digg-ar and the cloaked scout moved down the tunnel but just before it veered in another direction, they stopped. Digg-ar and his scout quickly turned their attention to the earth wall, while Mars kept watch.

Rolling up their sleeves, the two Mole-men attacked the tunnel wall with burly arms and strong flashing claws.

As they dug, an earth pile grew quickly in the existing passage and moments later, the pair disappeared from sight.

Stepping back into the main tunnel, Digg-ar motioned and Mars followed him into the new passage. As they proceeded, Digg-ar's scout remained behind to seal up the passage and rejoin his company.

"We're directly beneath Maliset and his Darkling army," Digg-ar telepathed, as the pair crept along on hands and knees. "Absolute silence is essential."

A few twists and turns later, Mars and Digg-ar halted their progress. While Digg-ar rose carefully, poking his head up through a small overhead opening, Mars took the opportunity to don his lightening boots.

"We're in position," he told Mars. "It's time for the signal, my young friend.

Mars and Digg-ar leaned forward and this time, pressed their temples together and touched their foreheads to the earthen wall. Their faces masks of pure concentration, they click-telepathed brief instructions to the Mole-commanders.

Seconds later, the pair emerged into an open meadow amid squawks of alarm from Maliset's legions of Darklings. Once again, the Mole-army had tunnelled undetected beneath the meadow and opened countless small cave-ins to briefly trap their foes.

"That may work briefly against my Darklings, young Marshall Shroom," Maliset's voice boomed, dripping with hatred. "But this time, you face me."

The night sky was suddenly ablaze with jagged arcs of brilliant crimson light, turning the battlefield as bright as high noon.

Turning swiftly they faced the evil one – his face contorted with fury... the air crackling with malevolent energy.

"It ends here, young Master Shroom," Maliset shrieked, swinging his fork-tipped staff toward the pair. "You have caused me enough trouble."

Pure hatred shining in his eyes, Maliset raised the staff and it trembled slightly before a thick, jagged bolt of red energy leapt from its forked tip, bucking and twisting through the air but heading for Mars.

His leather garment vibrating at full speed – the lethal ray was much more powerful than the lad had experienced when he first faced Maliset – Mars stood transfixed, like a moth before a candle flame.

"Move, Mars!" shouted Digg-ar, jumping toward his friend and shoving him fiercely aside.

As Mars fell, avoiding the lethal bolt by inches, he also quickly lost his momentary daze. Rolling himself into a ball and with an acrobatic flip he never knew he possessed, he regained his feet several feet away. Reaching into the leather garment Mars withdrew his own metal-tipped staff and turned to face his enemy.

That's when he saw Digg-ar, lying still on the ground… his cloak still smouldering from its encounter with Maliset's energy bolt.

"Digg-ar!" Mars screamed, and in a blur of movement, he knelt by his friend. Barely conscious, his face a mask of pain, Digg-ar waved Mars away.

"Leave me! Come back for me later. My injuries will be for nothing if Maliset once more gets you in his sights."

Realizing his friend was right, Mars became a blur of action, moving well away from his downed friend.

Maliset was just as quick. But with the two foes' rapid manoeuvres, Maliset was unable to get a solid sighting on Mars. More red bolts erupted from his staff, but Mars easily evaded them.

Pivoting quickly, Mars aimed his own staff at Maliset and jagged blue bolts of crackling energy shot toward his foe. Maliset quickly leapt behind a huge tree trunk and the blue bolt missed him.

"You'll not deny me my rightful destiny, young Mars," Maliset screamed, leaping out from behind the towering oak tree.

All around them came the sounds of hand-to-hand combat. Sturdy staffs clacked and smashed as Mole-men fought their former brothers, the Darklings.

High above them, the still dodging and weaving Marshall glimpsed a flying armada of Darkling-guided vultures heading swiftly toward the battle scene.

"All is lost if they start dropping their nets over our forces," Mars thought. He recalled with alarm his earlier, very close encounters with the nets.

Turning quickly toward the approaching vultures, he launched a flurry of arcing blue energy bolts into the sky. The malevolent flock pulled up in alarm.

"That'll slow them a bit but I have to find some way out of this… and quickly, before they're overhead!"

Taking in the full battle scene, Mars glanced up over Maliset and saw his chance.

Stopping quickly, he aimed his staff directly over Maliset's head, swiftly fired a strong blue energy bolt and resumed his evasive movements.

"Well wide of the mark, my young friend," Maliset taunted, loosing another volley of jagged red bolts at Mars, the discharges emitting a thunderous crackling sound.

Mars had counted on that, for the crackling discharge masked another sound that Maliset did not hear… until it was too late.

Overhead, a heavy oak limb, weakened by Mars' energy bolt, snapped and dropped like a stone on Maliset.

Screeching in fury, Maliset was knocked to the ground, his forked-tip staff flying end over end high into the air.

Shaking his head to clear it, Maliset gave a mighty shove to push the heavy limb aside and leaped to his feet... just in time to see Mars catch his errant staff... and level it – with the lad's own weapon – directly at him.

"That little snot-nose hasn't the nerve," Maliset thought to himself, reaching into his cloak.

Withdrawing long-bladed daggers from his cloak – one glimmering in each hand – Maliset raised his arms to launch them at Mars.

The metal ends of Mars' two staffs erupted with a crackle and energy bolts – red and blue – flashed across the distance between them.

Maliset's eyes grew wide with surprise. His sneering mouth gaped as the blue bolts struck and smashed both daggers and the red bolt smashed into his chest, toppling him backwards with great force.

Throwing down Maliset's staff, Mars approached his downed foe carefully; he knew the kind of duplicity Maliset was capable of and kept his own weapon at the ready. As he drew close, he could see that Maliset was defeated, dropped his own weapon and knelt beside him.

Pushing aside the evil one's hood, Mars watched in astonishment as Maliset transformed before his very eyes. Luxuriant red hair quickly grew, covering his once nearly bald and tattooed pate. The evil, coal-black eyes, barely visible behind heavy lids, became blue as they slowly focused on Mars.

Maliset's entire face – his entire being – softened and seemed to shrink slightly.

Mars cradled the man's head and shoulders as Maliset once more became Michael Shroom.

"I didn't..." he coughed, "didn't think you'd do it, my young nephew.

"But as you may have guessed, I'm glad you did," Michael wheezed. "I had embraced jealousy so long, it transformed me into a servant of evil... an easy convert to wickedness."

"You can't die now..." Mars interrupted, but was cut off by Michael's shakily raised hand.

Before him, Michael now began to age... and quickly. Red hair morphed to white as his smooth face rapidly wrinkled – eyebrows becoming two furry white caterpillars arching over the old man's eyes.

"You must be ever watchful," the old man whispered. "My master, the feral beast, is cunning; he won't take this battle as the final one. He, or a devious one of his choosing, will return... you must be ready.

"Your courage... your ingenuity... makes you... a formidable champion... a great protector of our people, nephew. Do not be sad. You have closed a long chapter... and given me peace... at last."

Exhaling a final breath, the faint light of life ebbed from Michael's eyes and Mars' great-many uncle slumped in his arms.

Gently laying Michael down, Mars slowly stood and turned to face the other combatants; both Mole-men and Darklings had stopped in awe when Maliset fell.

Glancing down once again, Mars drew back in surprise. What was briefly a young Michael and even more briefly an ancient uncle, had now turned to dust that was being blown away by errant wind currents. A single tear tracing a path down one cheek, Mars clicked: "Both sides... drop your weapons everyone! Nothing remains to divide us any longer."

26

Digg-ar's farewell

At Mars' order, Darklings and Mole-men threw down their weapons and lowered their hoods.

More odd transformations rippled across the field: The glowing red eyes that once identified the Darklings, dimmed and returned to the soft green of their former selves. It was as if a massive, collective trance lifted from the Darklings as they once more became Mole-people.

It started with one pair. Facing each other, the former foes grasped shoulders, leaned forward and touched foreheads. Soon the traditional gesture was repeated countless times among others across the expanse of the battlefield.

High above, the former Darklings guided their flying steeds to earth and leapt off to join the reconciliation. The vultures quickly took to the air and swiftly disappeared to the north.

Mars, watching in awe, suddenly remembered his fallen friend, rushed over and knelt by Digg-ar's side. Raising him in his arms, Mars leaned to touch foreheads with Digg-ar.

It wasn't fair, the 15-year-old thought. "I just got to know you, Digg-ar."

As warm orange-yellow sunlight penetrated the early dawn gloom to light the battlefield, a tear escaped the lad's eye, splashing onto the Mole-people leader's forehead. Digg-ar's eyes fluttered open, locking onto Mars' eyes.

"Do not mourn me, my young friend," the old man clicked softly. "My life has been long and rich."

The old man's eyes closed briefly, then slowly opened as the rising sun warmed him. With great effort, he turned his head to see his people and the former Darklings standing together.

"Seeing my people reunited before me is the greatest gift I could wish for," Digg-ar continued slowly. "For that I have you to thank. Our two peoples will always be friends.

"My people are together and safe from Maliset's evil. Now leave me, young Mars; you must return to Shroomville immediately. The Beast may already have become aware of his evil follower's defeat and death. My people will look after me now in our own traditional ways..."

Making a pillow of leaves and grass, Mars lay Digg-ar's head gently on it. In a final gesture of respect, Mars touched his forehead to Digg-ar's.

He stood, his wail of anguish echoing across the open plains. Shoulders sagging in sadness, the young man retrieved his staff, retracted it and returned it to its inside pocket.

He then found and took up Maliset's fork-tipped staff and, snapping it like a twig, scattered its splintered remains to the wind.

27

A costly victory

Mars' heart-rending howl cast a pall over the battlefield – now a reunion field – as Burr-oh rushed to his father's side.

As if in a trance, Mars trudged toward Windrush.

Events elsewhere, moved forward.

In Shroomville, the Constable had just completed his "serious talk" with Portia, who nodded in understanding. The pair then resumed the journey up the path to their mushroom homes, moving ever more quickly with anticipation.

There, before them, old Phinneus T. Phungi walked toward them, arms open and ready to embrace his lost friends.

Almost in sight of their families' familiar conical-roofed houses, the Constable stopped in his tracks. He gasped and fell to his knees, shoulders sagging.

"What's wrong, Constable?" Phungi asked, rushing toward him.

"What's happened?" Portia gasped. "Is Mars all right?"

"Yes, Portia," the Constable replied. "Mars is safe and they have won the day... but at great cost.

"Digg-ar was slain by Maliset when he pushed Mars aside to save him."

The Constable rose slowly to his feet and, arm around Portia and Phungi, the three continued their short walk.

Just as they approached the front door, it opened and there stood the Constable's thoroughly astounded wife.

"Marshall... Portia... you're safe!" she shouted. "You're home!"

Rushing into her husband's open arms, she suddenly realized someone was missing. Someone important.

"M-M-Mars... is he safe?" she stammered. "Where is he?"

"He's safe and he's on his way home as we speak," the Constable replied. "But two other friends need to see their daughter."

With that, three of them turned and walked to Portia's house – leaving Phungi alone – and moments later the Constable knocked on the door. It opened and Portia's parents stared out... dumbfounded.

Hugs and explanations followed in quick order. Just as quickly, the Bellas pulled their daughter inside and the Shrooms returned home to await their son.

As they neared their door, there was Phungi, dishevelled as always, waiting for them.

"He's safe and unhurt," Phungi shouted, holding his own small talk-mirror.

"We have lost our good friend Digg-ar, but the menace of Maliset is no more," the old man continued.

"Though come to think of it, young Mars seemed strangely conflicted by the evil one's death…"

"Come inside, Phinneas," Mrs. Shroom said, holding the door open for him. "I'll put on some tea while we wait for Mars."

Again, the door had barely closed when the sound of running footsteps was heard.

"I'd recognize those footsteps anywhere," said Phungi. "If I'm not mistaken, your son has returned."

Moments later, Mars burst past the thick fern cluster at the side of the house and ran to his mother's open arms.

It was perhaps the best hug Mars had ever received from his mother… and probably the best one he'd given her. Soon, Mrs. Shroom held her son at arm's length, but this time, her eyes widened with alarm.

"Mars... your hair!" she spluttered. "Part of it's gone completely white! What happened?"

Sure enough, at the centre of his forehead there started a shock-white lock of hair that formed a strange pattern through the lad's carrot red hair. It's shape... a lightening bolt.

"That's a story for another time, Mother," Mars smiled back at her. "Let me just say... our, er, adventures were hair-raising.

"What I'm interested in right now is something to eat," Mars added. "I feel like I haven't eaten for days..."

More tears. More hugs and finally, the Shrooms and their guest filed inside.

28

Shroomville returns to normal… or does it?

The next morning, Mars awoke in his own familiar bed, wearing his comfortable old pyjamas under soft, warm blankets.

Warm, yellow sunshine bathed his room as Mars stirred and stretched, willing himself to wakefulness.

Sweeping blankets aside, Mars swung his feet over the side and sat on the edge of his bed. He smiled as he took in his comforting surroundings, stretching and yawning in the warm morning sun. His recent adventure seemed almost a dream.

A similar scene unfolded in the Bella house as Portia too, stirred and awoke. Still half asleep, her mind wrestled with what seemed to her to be a long nightmare.

Almost as one, the two youngsters stood, rubbing sleepy eyes. Mars opened his closet door to draw out the day's clothing while Portia dug into her top drawer.

There, before Mars, hung the soft leather jerkin with its many secret pockets. There, atop Portia's neatly folded cotton blouse, rested the stone amulet Mars had given her when they parted outside Murkwood Forest.

As Mars reached to touch the butter-soft leather, Portia grasped the amulet. Both objects pulsed gently in response to their owners' touch.

"It wasn't a dream," the youths mind-spoke in unison. "It did happen!"

"Yes," came Marshall Senior's telepathic voice. "And remember our discussion, Portia. These gifts, our abduction, the escape and the battle are ours alone to know – as is our ability to mind-speak.

"Remember. If anyone asks, Portia, you became lost and were taken in by some kindly forest people," he continued. "It took me all this time to find you but my accidental fall delayed our return. That's when Mars took up the search and here we all are, back in Shroomville, safe and sound."

"Yes indeed," chimed in old Phungi's sleepy voice. "Our little secret... especially at this early hour in the morning."

Mars and Portia smiled and went on with the morning's familiar routine. They looked forward to spending the summer together.

Elsewhere in the Shroom house, Mars' mother stood before the kitchen window, preparing to start the morning meal. She swept aside the curtains and was bathed in warm sunshine. About to turn and retrieve some dishes from a cupboard, she paused abruptly. A ghost of a smile crinkling her face, Mrs. Shroom murmured aloud to herself:

"Yes... our little secret..."

****

About the author

Ron Dennis is a former daily journalist and seasoned corporate communicator who has been writing in one form or another for nearly four decades. In addition to newspapering and corporate public relations, Ron has also written, edited and taken photographs for several corporate newsletters.

He has created countless marketing communication pieces, including sales brochures and company background/capabilities pieces, and has crafted speeches for senior government ministers and corporate executives.

In recent years, Ron has turned his hand to writing fiction and has signed an agreement with the Hamilton Spectator and Newspapers In Education to serialize *Adventures in Shroomville.*

Manor House
905-648-2193
www.manor-house.biz